*Books by Adrienne Richard*

PISTOL

THE ACCOMPLICE

WINGS

# ❧ WINGS ❧

# ꧁ WINGS ꧂

BY

ADRIENNE RICHARD

*AN ATLANTIC MONTHLY PRESS BOOK*

LITTLE, BROWN AND COMPANY

BOSTON     TORONTO

FIRST EDITION

T 10/74

"The Ballad of John Silver" from POEMS of John Masefield (Copy-
right 1916 by John Masefield, renewed 1944 by John Masefield)
reprinted by permission of The Society of Authors as the literary
representative of the Estate of John Masefield and The Macmillan
Publishing Co., Inc.

LIBRARY OF CONGRESS CATALOGING IN PUBLICATION DATA

Richard, Adrienne.
  Wings.

  "An Atlantic Monthly Press book."
  [1. United States—Social life and customs—
1918–1945—Fiction] I. Title.
PZ7.R378Wi    [Fic]     74-12439
ISBN 0-316-74321-6

ATLANTIC-LITTLE, BROWN BOOKS
ARE PUBLISHED BY
LITTLE, BROWN AND COMPANY
IN ASSOCIATION WITH
THE ATLANTIC MONTHLY PRESS

*Published simultaneously in Canada*
*by Little, Brown & Company (Canada) Limited*

PRINTED IN THE UNITED STATES OF AMERICA

This book is given in memory of my mother, Marguerite Gooder

# Contents

# ❧ WINGS ❧

# 🖼 1 🖼

## Pip

**P**IP WAITED while the tarantula crossed the drive, marveling at its bigness. The hairy brown-black body was as large as the palm of her hand, and the slender, arched, hairy legs carried the body like a saucer. As she watched, the spider stepped daintily and silently over the blacktopped drive.

Her brother Parkman stuck his head out an upstairs window and yelled, "What are you waiting for? I told you to hurry."

"I'm waiting till the tarantula gets across the driveway."

"Where is it? Oh, now I see it. Look out. They can jump three feet right in the air."

On delicate legs the tarantula picked its way to the edge of the drive and disappeared into the grass.

Then Pip went around to the front of her wagon, spun an imaginary propeller while she made a noise — rhum-rhum. The propeller stuck at first, and then it got going. She ducked under the imaginary wing and climbed into the wagon, sitting on one knee and keeping the other leg out for a brake. Whispering, "Contact, contact, let 'er go!" she pulled the string tied to the wooden blocks under the front wheels, set them in the wagon behind her, took the tongue firmly in hand, and with one push coasted gently down the drive and into the road.

At the end of the drive she guided the wagon to the right, downhill. She scanned the sky for other planes, friend or foe. Bill Tanner leaned from his milk truck and waved as he passed going the other way. She saluted formally. He was not a friend, but he was to be respected.

The wagon glided on, picking up speed around the bend leading toward the village. There the road climbed a slight grade which brought the wagon to a halt. Pip got out, marked the place on the blacktop with a piece of white chalk she carried in her overalls pocket for the purpose, and, taking the tongue in hand, pulled the wagon behind her.

When she had gone around the hill, she came out on the main street of the little town, a street which ran straight past the post office to the other end of the village. She could see the bottom edge of Bemis the Baker's signboard six blocks away. The bell in the post office tower rang a deep, regular ten o'clock.

"You'd better get out of the street, Pip," the mailman called out. "Come up on the sidewalk. It's safer. How are you today?"

"I'm fine," she said. She smelled the sweat on his shirt and the leather of his mailbag as she passed him.

At the post office corner she turned into the side street, passed some small shops, and pulled her wagon into the open arcade of the Valley Paramount, the biggest little picture show in the valley. So it said on the sign, and she believed it.

After she put the wooden blocks in front of the wagon wheels, she studied the shiny photographs in the display windows. Rin Tin Tin was a Coming Attraction. One picture showed the great German police dog leaping over a prison wall. Another showed Clara Bow, the "It" girl. Tom Mix smiled a big smile under his ten-gallon white hat while his black and white cow pony reared. They were Next. Now the feature was Greta Garbo, who had the biggest eyes Pip had ever seen.

When she had given all the pictures thorough study, she knocked on the office door and held her breath. The door opened. A cloud of steam scented with eucalyptus oil boiled through the doorway, and out of it appeared a small round, bald man with a wheeze for a voice. Pip released her breath.

"Hello, Mr. Zick."

"Hallo, Pip, how's tricks?"

"I'm fine, Mr. Zick. Are you all right today?"

"No worse, Pip, no worse."

"It must be terrible not being able to breathe."

"So long as I live like a Delphic oracle in this cloud of steam, I can make the old wind bags work."

"Maybe your hay fever will go away when it starts to rain."

"Then my asthma will get worse. I came to this place to be high and dry, for my health. I should have stayed in Brooklyn. It was no worse."

"Do you eat the right things, Mr. Zick? Bemis the Baker told my mother his lima bean bread cured somebody of something, I forget what."

"Lima bean bread? This I must try. Well, how goes it with you, little pippin? So you go back to school next week. No more overalls, no more boys' gym shoes. You'll have to get your hair cut, I suppose." He patted her head. "A curly nest, if I ever saw one. Can you comb it?"

"It's hard." Pip lifted one toe and rubbed the white rubber circle on the inside ankle of her gym shoe. "Do you think I'll have to get it cut?"

"Who knows? What does Mama say?"

"She hasn't said anything, and I don't have any dresses except old ones."

"Maybe overalls are all right then. Mama knows." He thumped his chest to help draw a breath. "You want Parkman's collection? You should go into the trash business. You could make money."

"I'll help you, Mr. Zick."

She followed him into the office which was so filled with steam that she had to fan the air to see anything. The old oak desk was cluttered with papers, and the yellow-brown chair was very old. She spun it on its swivel, going by.

"Don't take too many, little sweetheart. Two trips with small loads."

Mr. Zick carried some, and she carried more of the shiny black and white publicity pictures and put them in the wagon. When they had made two stacks even with the top of the wagon, Pip said, "I guess that's all I can take, Mr. Zick."

"Tell Parkman there's more where those came from. A big boy like that should fetch his own."

"Oh, I don't mind, Mr. Zick. He gives me all the airplane pictures."

"Well, that's a fair deal. I think there are some this time, Pip. I ran three airplane movies while you were away this summer."

"Oh, did you, Mr. Zick? Were they good ones?"

"In one there were biplanes all over the sky. It was about aviators and dogfights in the last war. Richard Arlen — he was the hero. They had the movie cameras right up in the sky with them. You could see their faces in the open cockpits."

"Did they salute when they went by?"

"Every time, they made the salute. In one scene a plane crashed. It fell burning in a tailspin. I have never seen anything like it in a movie, or in real life, to tell the truth. *Wings* it was called. *Wings* — only one word —" He passed his hand through the air before their eyes. "*Wings* — you'd love it, Pip."

"Will it ever come back, Mr. Zick? Do you think I'll ever see it?"

"You'd like to see it?" Mr. Zick studied her face through the eucalyptus steam. "You'd like to see it. Let me think. I've got Garbo and Bow and Mix and — let me try. Maybe by Christmas, maybe in January I can bring it back. I'll try. For you I'll try."

"Oh, Mr. Zick, you're wonderful!"

"Of course I am, of course." He wheezed with laughter. "You get in. I'll play contact for you."

Pip knelt in the wagon, this time on both knees, and gripped the tongue like a joystick. She leaned over the side and signed to Mr. Zick. With some effort he gripped the propeller, made a try, and finally got it spinning.

"Contact, let 'er go!" Pip said.

Mr. Zick pulled the blocks from the wheels and stepped back. As the wagon coasted by him, he made the salute. Pip returned it, this time the salute to the respected friend. Mr. Zick dropped the blocks on top of the show pictures as Pip guided the wagon out onto the sidewalk.

It didn't go far, only the distance allowed by the momentum from the slanted arcade. Before she reached the corner, she had to get out and start pulling. The pictures were heavy, and the way home seemed much farther. The sun was higher and hotter, but some of the shops had awnings for shade. Beyond the shops she pressed close to the shrubs and trees which overhung the dirt sidewalk, but still she felt her hair getting wet and curling tighter. Water ran down past her ears in a little trickle.

She took the other way around the hill. There was an avenue of acacia trees that way which shaded the sides of the road. When she reached the saddle of the hill, she climbed in the wagon again, one knee under her, one leg out for braking. From there she coasted smoothly in the acacia shade around the bend downhill to the driveway and part way up on sheer momentum. She marked the place where the wagon stopped with the chalk. It was not so far as the last time. The pictures must be heavier, more of them. Parkman had told her that she would glide farther if the wagon weighed more. Then it had more traction. But he was wrong.

"You took long enough," Parkman yelled, leaning out the upstairs window. "Is that all he had?"

"He has stacks and stacks. He saved them all summer."

"You could have brought more."

"I didn't want to sit on them."

"You could have pulled. Now what are you doing?"

"I'm sorting out the airplane pictures."

"Boy, you'd better not take any others. You take one Douglas Fairbanks and I'll —" He vanished from the window and in half a minute shot out the front door.

"I don't want one Douglas Fairbanks," Pip said.

Parkman snatched the pictures from her hands, went through them and pushed them back at her. "You'd better not." He sat down in the wagon and began looking through the piles of photographs. They were hot and shiny in the sun. "The turtle fell off the garage roof again."

"He doesn't want to stay up there, Parkman. Maybe it's too hot."

"Turtles like it hot."

"I think he wants to go back to the water."

"The tub is full of water up there."

"It's kind of green."

"Turtles like it green. Here—two airplanes." Pip added them to her collection. She found a picture of Al Wilson, the Daredevil of the Sky, and laid it on the top to study. Just then the kitchen screen door creaked and banged. Mrs. Hernandez the cook had come out, her brown face sad and set. She wore her gray button sweater and Pip's mother's last year's hat with the brim turned back so Pip knew Mrs. Hernandez was leaving them — and right before lunch.

The screen banged quickly again, and Pip's mother was right behind Mrs. Hernandez, saying, "I really think, Mrs. Hernandez —" but Mrs. Hernandez did not wait to hear what Pip's mother really thought. "One bite from that spider, and I die!" she exclaimed. "I will not stay here unless you do something about that tarantula."

"I really don't like to kill anything," Pip's mother said, "but if you will stay . . ."

"Only — only —" Mrs. Hernandez raised her hand. "I stay only if the tarantula goes."

"But he's gone," Pip said. "I saw him go this morning."

Mrs. Hernandez shook her head. "He went into the grass. He is still alive." Pip started for the edge of the drive to see for herself, but Mrs. Hernandez caught her arm. Surprised, Pip pulled free while her mother said, "Please, Mrs. Hernandez, I think Parkman can do something after lunch. Can you wait till then? You know my sister is coming and bringing a friend, and I do want everything to be just right, the way you do it. If you would consider waiting till later —"

Mrs. Hernandez muttered something, but no one heard her for the noise at the foot of the driveway.

"Oh, for heaven's sake," Pip's mother cried, "here they are now."

Mrs. Hernandez had to turn back to the kitchen because a large motorcycle with a sidecar blocked the drive.

# ◉ 2 ◉

## Radyar

**P**IP HAD NEVER SEEN a motorcycle before, not one that
she could touch. Once at the Saturday afternoon matinee
in Mr. Zick's movie house she had watched Rin Tin Tin,
the great dog, ride in a sidecar while his master, a World
War officer, drove the machine right through a barbed wire
barricade. It had never occurred to her that just such a motorcycle would come toward her up her own driveway as it was
doing now.

Aunt Andrea, her mother's sister, was seated in the sidecar, wearing a helmet and goggles and an orange and yellow scarf trailing like flame from her throat. With a roar
the motorcycle came to a stop within touching distance.
Aunt Andrea rose from the sidecar, lifting the little round
goggles. Her yellow hair sprang up in ringlets all about her
face as she peeled the helmet from her head. "Dorrit darling!" she cried. "Parkman! Pip! Sweethearts, you're back
at last. Welcome to Paradise!"

Leaping out, Aunt Andrea gave Parkman a hug, making
him stiff and embarrassed. She took Pip's face in her hands
and kissed her lips, but Pip paid no attention. She could

not take her eyes off the man on the motorcycle. He looked exactly like an aviator.

After adjusting this and that on the handlebars of the motorcycle, the man sat back with his legs thrust forward and surveyed the scene. He wore riding breeches and leather puttees like the ones they wore in the World War and a leather helmet and small round goggles. It was exactly like the costume Al Wilson, the Daredevil of the Sky, wore in the photograph she held in her hand. Her chest contracted suddenly. Could this be the real Al Wilson? Was Al Wilson her Aunt Andrea's new friend?"

While Pip studied him, the man studied the white stucco house, his eyes going from the dark front door to the great oak shading the garage roof to Pip's wagon to Mrs. Hernandez who stood with one hand on the kitchen doorknob to Parkman, sullen and angry as he gripped his collection of pictures, to the two sisters who held each other at arm's length, laughing, and finally to Pip. When his gaze came to rest on her, he smiled with a great flashing of white teeth, removed his goggles and pulled off the helmet. His black hair lay flat and wet against his head. Pip's chest relaxed as her heart sank. He was not Al Wilson, the Daredevil of the Sky. He dropped the helmet in the sidecar and stepped off the machine.

"Dorrit, this is Radyar!" cried Aunt Andrea. "He is in the star business." She went off into peals of laughter which Radyar ignored.

"So you are the lovely Dorrit I have heard so much

about." Radyar took Pip's mother's hand in both of his and held it while he flashed his smile again. Pip noticed that his hands were much bigger than her mother's and he wore a shiny silver wristwatch as big as her grandfather's pocket watch. It flashed in the sun.

"And this is Parkman," Aunt Andrea said. "For heaven's sake, Parkman, don't be so stiff. He won't bite."

Parkman, shaking Radyar's hand, mumbled and turned red and fixed his eyes on Radyar's left puttee.

"And, last but not least, Ann Margaret."

"My name is Pip." As she held out her hand, her face and her voice were grave.

Immediately Radyar's smile disappeared, and his face too became serious. "And mine is Radyar." He took her hand in his, and they shook. Pip wondered if she had at last touched the person of a real aviator, and she put her hand carefully into her pocket as if it held something she didn't want to lose. All the while she never let her eyes leave Radyar's face.

Dorrit, her mother, urged them toward the house, welcoming them and explaining how she hoped to have lunch out on the porch, but just as they arrived, she had been in the midst of persuading Mrs. Hernandez the cook not to quit at that very moment, and consequently she had no idea whether there would be any lunch at all, even though Mrs. Huckaby had sent over a very special dish.

Aunt Andrea's laughter rang through the living room. "Oh — oh, I can guess what that means. Radyar will love it."

"At this moment of extreme hunger," Radyar said, "I would love anything." While he spoke, Pip watched him scan the room: the beamed ceiling, the great stone fireplace, the bright pillows on the wicker sofas, the long windows shuttered against the midday sun. "Such a pleasant room," he murmured.

At that moment Mrs. Hernandez emerged from the kitchen bearing a great tray of melon cups. She carried it out onto the terrace.

"Oh, Dorrit, you won!" Aunt Andrea whispered.

Pip slipped into the bathroom under the stairs. It was a dark bathroom with no outside window, and a cockroach lived there so that she always looked before she went in. She was not afraid of cockroaches. They couldn't hurt you, but they caught you by surprise and they ran awfully fast. You were never sure which way. She washed her face carefully with suds on her hands and afterwards wiped her whole head with the towel. It was too late to go upstairs and change coveralls. The ones she was wearing weren't too dirty, and she looked more like an aviatrix because they were a little soiled.

The blue table on the terrace stood in the shade of the Mexican trumpet vine, and everyone was gathering around it when Pip appeared. The chair legs scraped across the stone as the chairs were pulled up, and the great white napkins were flicked to the side and spread across laps, like sails coming down. Parkman stuck his napkin behind his belt buckle, and Pip stuffed one corner of hers in between two red buttons below the edge of the table. While she dipped her spoon into the cold ginger ale bubbling around the red and green melon balls, she watched Radyar. He picked up his bowl and drank the ginger ale to the last drop. "Refreshing after a long, dry ride," he said.

"Dorrit, you'll have another admirer if you don't watch out." Aunt Andrea tossed her yellow curls, laughing gaily. Parkman didn't lift his eyes from his fruit as he ate it, clacking the spoon on the bottom of the bowl.

While Pip studied him, Radyar looked off beyond the terrace. "This is a lovely place — these beautiful trees. Look at that magnificent sycamore. The white bark almost shines in this light. The way those branches spread out makes it look like an animal, and all those bumps and nobs like healed-over wounds. Magnificent!"

"Now you will make a big hit with Pip!" cried Aunt Andrea. "That is her favorite place to play."

Pip did not say anything. There were people who could be trusted with where she played and what she played there and those who could not. Tipping up her fruit bowl to drink the last drops, she watched Radyar over the rim. He was looking at the sycamore and nodding as he murmured, "I can see why."

When her mother rang a little silver bell that stood by her plate, Mrs. Hernandez came out with another tray. She cleared away the fruit bowls and set a plate before each person. On the plate was a slice of something that looked like meat loaf, a runny black gravy and a mound of spinach.

"Oh, this is Mrs. Huckaby's main dish," Aunt Andrea laughed. "I know what this is."

"What?" Parkman asked.

"It's nut loaf and it's very good," Dorrit said.

"What's the black stuff?"

"It's Savita gravy."

"Why's it black?"

"It's made from black molasses and soybeans and I don't know what, but it's very good."

"I don't like black food."

"I expected that." Dorrit rang the little silver bell again. Without being told Mrs. Hernandez brought a plate with a chicken sandwich. Dorrit gave her a sad, knowing smile as she exchanged the plates in front of Parkman.

"I don't disrespect Parkman's aesthetic judgment," Radyar said, "but I find the nut loaf, black gravy and all, fit for the gods and goddesses of this valley."

"Radyar will have this household charmed before dessert," Aunt Andrea teased in a cascade of laughter. "And look at Pip's plate. She has eaten it all."

"It was delicious," Pip said, although she didn't like anyone to mention her plate. It sounded too much like what was said to reluctant eaters, and she wanted to change the subject. "The scorpions are back in Mrs. Huckaby's bathtub."

Aunt Andrea shrieked with laughter, crying, "Oh, Pip, the things you say!" sending an angry, hot flush to Pip's face. What was so funny? Parkman didn't think it was funny. He looked at Aunt Andrea in mild surprise. Her mother dabbed her lips with the napkin. And Radyar turned his bright blue eyes on her. He was smiling a little as he said, "I have a great affinity for scorpions. The scorpion is my birth sign."

"Oh, so that is the star business you are in," Dorrit said. "Are you Radyar the astrologer? I see that name everyday in Madame Solar's newspaper horoscopes?"

Radyar, smiling, admitted that it was he, and Aunt Andrea exclaimed, "Radyar is Madame Solar's disciple, her fair-haired boy." Smoothing his black hair, Radyar laughed, his eyes narrowing and flashing. "It is more accurate to say I am her trainee."

Pip watched Radyar carefully, wondering if an astrologer was some kind of aviator and puzzling over a way to find out without sending Aunt Andrea into laughing shrieks again. By the time she finished her dessert, she had made up her mind.

"Mr. Radyar, can I have a ride on your motorcycle?"

"Of course! Good idea! We will go right now and leave these two, Merry Laughter and your mother, to share their separate summers while we explore the great world. How about you, Parkman? Pip can ride behind me, and you can have the sidecar."

"I have to kill the tarantula," Parkman said, and Radyar narrowed his bright eyes again. "So there are vipers in this paradise, are there? Come along, Pip, we two shall see the world." He strode through the house with Pip hurrying behind. His hard leather heels cracked against the tile floor.

The motorcycle radiated heat in spite of the shade. Pip felt the hot seat through her coveralls as she settled into the white sidecar. Radyar handed her Aunt Andrea's helmet.

"Can I wear it?"

"You must!" He helped her stuff her tight curls inside, pulled the flaps down over her ears and set the goggles over her eyes. The band was too long. He shortened it and patted the goggles into place. "There! You look perfect. Just like an aviatrix. A perfect aviatrix!"

Pip lifted her face and smiled, and Radyar, watching her, said, "Ah, so you would like to be an aviatrix, I knew it, I knew it. I felt the vibration." Then he set the engine roaring, settled himself astride his machine and took them down the drive. At the end he looked both ways and asked, "Where shall we go? Do you know a way up into the mountains? Take me up to the hills."

Gravely Pip signaled to turn left. As the motorcycle passed under the acacia trees, she peered over the edge of the sidecar. A cockpit was just like this, she was certain. Lifting her face to the sky, she scanned it for biplanes and monoplanes. When the road emerged from the oak grove, she made certain the skies were clear above the brown grass golf course. As the motorcycle roared up the winding road, she felt the exposure to the sun and wind and the suggestion of danger. Sweat sprang from her scalp under the leather helmet.

Radyar piloted his machine along the brows of the foothills, roaring into the U-turns as the road went upwards. On the crest of one hill where two twisted trees shaded a lookout he turned off the road and brought the motorcycle to a halt in the shade. He stripped the helmet from his head and drew a deep breath. Pip did the same, wiping sweat from her temples. The entire valley spread out before them, and Radyar raised his arms toward it. "How beautiful! How beautiful!" he exclaimed.

Pip looked down at the road they had just come over, all the switchbacks visible like black hairpins lying on the edges of the hills. The brown fairways of the golf course made a pattern like a maze, and beyond that the leafy branches of the trees covered the valley like a roof. Pointing to them, Pip said, "Our house is in there."

Radyar asked her about this landmark and that one, and she pointed out the road that went into the mountains to the hot springs where you could swim and never turn blue no matter how long you stayed in the water and the road that led the other way to Los Angeles and Hollywood, the bell tower on the post office which rang all night long when there was a brush fire in the mountains and fire fighters were needed, and the long tin roof reflecting the sun which covered the chutes and conveyor belts of the orange-packing plant. The last thing she told him about was the great stone cliff which faced them from the far end of the valley. "It turns red when the sun goes down," she said.

"Magnificent," Radyar murmured.

In the silence that followed Pip summoned her question. "Mr. Radyar?"

"Not Mister Radyar please. Simply — Radyar!" He made it sound like the name of a magician.

"Radyar, is a strol — is a — what is a strol —" She had forgotten the word, and angry with herself, she flushed.

"An astrologer?" His eyes remained steady on the far cliffs, and her cheeks cooled. "An astrologer reads the stars."

He did not fly airplanes then. Pip was silent, thinking.

"It is a very ancient art, three thousand, four thousand years old. We do not know when it began, but long ago when men knew the stars and the sky and the sun and the moon and the planets and the directions and the seasons in the ancient ways. Now those ways are lost — lost, except for a few of us who practice the ancient art. We know, we know. You see, Pip, the stars move, the stars and the planets and the moon and earth, and they are in certain places when you are born. It is where they are when you are born that determines your horoscope."

"My what?"

"It is a chart to guide your life. I draw up horoscopes for people. I have made them for movie stars, for Aunt Andrea of the cascading giggles. Horoscopes are my business." He rested one hand on his chest and looked at Pip. "Would you like me to do your horoscope?"

She nodded.

"When is your birthday? No — no, don't tell me — let me guess." Radyar looked at her closely. His bright blue eyes glittered sharply. "You were born — yes, I am certain — you were born in July or August."

Pip was astonished. "August 15!"

Radyar laughed aloud and slapped his riding breeches. "I knew it. You are a Leo. You were born under the sun sign of the lion, a great sign, a great sign!" He looked off across the valley. "Ah, the Leos. They have great courage and imagination and daring and loyalty and stubbornness and prideful anger."

Stubborn and proud, that's what her father had said when she told him she didn't like baby dolls or dolls at all. "You are the most stubborn little kid I have ever known," he had snapped. "All little girls like dolls. If your mother had given you one, you would know." "I don't want one," she had cried, but he had made her take it. Pip's smile had faded away.

"There are always good things and bad things under each sign," said Radyar. "It is nothing to worry about — being stubborn or proud or angry. Your sun sign helps you to know yourself. Think of it — to have courage and imagination and nerve and strong feelings. Everything about a Leo is strong." Radyar spread his arms wide. "So you see, Pip, two or three aspects not so good but the others magnificent."

Still she was not reassured.

"An aviatrix should be a Leo."

Her upturned face brightened again.

"She should be — a woman who rises in the air and leaves the earth and all we have known behind, all man has ever known — she must be a Leo."

Surely it was true. Radyar said so, and she believed him.

To cast her horoscope he needed to know what time she was born, which she couldn't tell him, and where, which she could — in Kansas City, Missouri. He laughed. "Not so beautiful a place as this valley."

[22]

The words, Kansas City, opened a tiny door inside her, and through it a sensation like boiling water flowed suddenly. Feeling it, Pip was silent.

"The next time we meet, I will have your horoscope and I will tell you what it means." Radyar stood up and stepped down on the starter several times before the motor roared. Then he settled back on the saddle. Pip put on her helmet and adjusted the goggles. When she was ready, he turned the motorcycle into the road and returned over the switchbacks to her house.

That night Pip lay in the white iron bed on the sleeping porch and through the dark sycamore boughs watched the stars. They were large and bright and shone with a white light in the black sky. She waited to see them move.

"Parkman?"

Her brother rolled over in the next bed. "What?"

"Parkman, Radyar's going to tell my horoscope."

"Boy, you're really dumb," Parkman said. "You believe anything."

Pip felt her head go hot. "You don't even know what a horoscope is!" she cried.

"I do, too. It's supposed to be your fortune from the stars. He's just a fortune teller, like somebody at a carnival."

"He is not! Aunt Andrea had hers made. Radyar did one for her!"

"So what? She told Mother she didn't believe a word of it."

"She did not!"

"She did, too. I heard her, after you left. He's a big fake."

"He is not!"

"Aunt Andy said he's a fortune hunter, too."

"Well! you can't tell fortunes if you don't find them first."

"Not that kind of fortune, dummy. She said he wants to marry somebody with lots of money."

"He does not!" Pip cried out.

"How do you know?" Parkman jeered. "Aunt Andy knows more than you do. Besides, I'll bet Radyar isn't even his real name."

"It is so."

"How do you know?"

Pip turned away and stared out into the night. She didn't know, but she believed Radyar. He wouldn't lie to her. She fixed her eyes on a star among the branches. She wanted to see it move.

"If he can tell your fortune from the stars, he'll tell you when you're going to die," Parkman said.

For a moment Pip could not catch her breath. Her scalp prickled with fright. She didn't want to know when she was going to die. She wasn't ever going to.

"Oh, well, what do you care?" said Parkman. "Everybody dies sometime."

"You will, too, then, Parkman."

"See? You're scared. You believe anything."

Pip turned her back to Parkman's bed and squeezed her eyes shut as quickly as she could. Still it was not fast enough to avoid catching sight of one star through the sycamore tree. She wondered if it had moved, but now she didn't want to know.

# 🌀 3 🌀

## The Blue Dress

EARLY MORNING held the world in a delicate golden net when Pip awoke. Parkman was still asleep in the next bed with the covers over his head. Beyond him, in the bed by the door, her mother had covered her head, too. Only a hank of red-brown hair showed on the pillow. After a moment the racket which had wakened her began again.

A woodpecker drummed on the tile roof right over her head, making a sound so tremendous Pip stuck her fingers in her ears, but it was no use. The woodpecker was determined to pound his head off. Just when she could stand it no longer, the noise stopped and he flew through the trees to a telephone pole. There he began hammering again on the metal transformer which hung like a great garbage can on the crosstree. The noise was farther away but more piercing.

Pip felt a lump rising in her stomach and her spirits clouded. She didn't believe everything, the way Parkman said, and she wasn't afraid of dying. Not knowing what it meant or what it felt like bothered her. She was troubled by not knowing what a fortune hunter was and whether Radyar was what he said he was. She needed to plan how to find out without being jeered at. Not everyone could be trusted. She threw back her covers and got up.

Inside the house it was very still. She padded on bare feet along the hall to her room. It was not a bedroom, since her bed was on the sleeping porch. It was like a large dressing room with a closet and a chest of drawers built into one wall, a wicker chair with a red bandanna-print cushion and a small desk by the window which looked out on the garage roof.

Pip sat down at her desk in her nightgown and took up the airplane pictures which lay there. She looked at them, she divided them into piles, the ones she liked and the ones she didn't like much and the ones she wasn't sure about, but her feelings would not follow her eyes. Inside she felt a knot.

She looked across the hall into Parkman's room. His room was like hers with a wardrobe and a chest, a desk and a wicker chair with a blue bandanna cushion. Parkman's clothes lay in little heaps like drop cookies on the floor. The big, square-cornered leather suitcase which had held his things on the way from Kansas City stood open, with his clothes still in it rummaged into a tangle. His collection of photographs had spilled off his desk. While she thought a moment, Pip heard the back door open and Mrs. Hernandez moving about. She padded downstairs and into the kitchen.

Mrs. Hernandez had draped her gray sweater over the back of a kitchen chair and was lighting the front gas burner on the marbled blue stove. Shaking the match till it was out, she smiled at Pip who sat down in the chair and yawned like a cavern.

"You are up too early again," said Mrs. Hernandez.

"The woodpecker came back."

"He should be shot," said Mrs. Hernandez.

"Parkman tried it day before yesterday, but he missed. He used a whole box of beebees."

"And what if he hit him? There is more than one woodpecker in this world."

Pip watched her carefully as Mrs. Hernandez filled the tea kettle with water and set it over the heat and took milk from the icebox, poured some into a pan and placed it on the other front burner. "Mrs. Hernandez."

"Yes, little serious one."

"Mrs. Hernandez, what's a fortune hunter?"

Mrs. Hernandez stirred sugar and cocoa into the warming milk. "He is a pirate. He sails on a big ship and steals gold from good people. I know because many pirates were Spanish people like me, but now they are only in the moving pictures — thank the good God. Aye-yie. Come along. You can have your breakfast on the terrace." Thinking that Radyar did not fit this description, Pip followed her. Mrs. Hernandez had brought fresh lima bean bread from the bakery on her way to work, and now she had toasted and buttered two thick slices to go with Pip's hot cocoa. They were so good that Pip asked her for a third slice. Before she finished, her mother came to the table, Mrs. Hernandez following her with a tray of morning coffee.

Her mother sat down, put her elbows on the table and

bowed her head. The upturning curls of her red-brown hair swung forward over her hands. "That woodpecker," she sighed. "Oh, if Parkman could only shoot straight! Why is there always something unpleasant in this world?" She sat back, sighing again.

"He's stopped now," Pip said. "He flew away a little while ago."

"As soon as I got up," said her mother. "As soon as he knew we were all awake."

"Except Parkman."

"Oh, he's awake too. He must be." She poured a cup of coffee and added hot milk and sat back in her chair. "Next week it won't matter so much. You two will be getting up for school. Oh, Pip, I can't believe it. You are growing up so fast."

Pip continued to eat her toast and looked out beyond the shaded terrace to the brown grass and the sycamore tree. In her mind she saw the faces of classmates she had not seen all summer. They did not seem the least familiar nor did she seem familiar reflected in their wide blank eyes. The teacher would be a stranger. Without knowing she did it, she ran her hand over her curly hair.

"It wouldn't hurt to take a little off," her mother said. "It would be easier to comb."

"I hardly ever comb it." Her mother fell silent, watching her over her cup. They sat for several minutes without speaking.

"Mother." Her mother waited. "Is Radyar going to marry Aunt Andy?"

Her mother smiled. "Whatever gave you that idea?"

"Parkman said Radyar wants to marry someone with lots of money. Aunt Andy said so."

"Oh, Andy thinks every man is after her money."

"Are they going to get married?"

"Not that I know of, darling. Why?"

Pip fell silent, but the knot inside her loosened a little. After a while her mother said, "Whatever will you wear to school, Pip? You haven't a dress to your name, not one that fits."

"I don't like dresses," Pip said.

"Coveralls are much better," Dorrit murmured. "I'm sure the school wouldn't object even though the other girls are wearing dresses."

Pip stirred uneasily. Marjorie Steadman who had almost white hair always wore yellow dresses with white collars and cuffs, and she stayed clean all day. She didn't even wrinkle very much. The picture of Marjorie in her mind brought up a feeling of disgust. She, Pip, was not Marjorie Steadman, and she didn't want to be like her, at least most of the time she didn't. But still, if she wore coveralls and Marjorie wore her yellow dress — Pip bit her lip.

"It has to be blue," Pip said, "and it has to have buttons in front. And it has to have a belt."

Her mother smiled. "Go get the box from the chest by the front door," she said.

Pip slipped from her chair with half a glance toward her mother. A slight suspicion that she had been led into a trap passed through her. Sometimes she didn't like what her mother did, but she never guessed until too late that she was being tricked.

The interior of the house was still dark. The shutters were closed on the eastern windows, and the heavy front door was shut. She hadn't seen the box when she came downstairs, but it may not have been there. Her mother could have brought it down when she came. Pip's sense of suspicion increased.

Pip carried the flat, rectangular cardboard box onto the terrace. She lifted the lid. With a rustle layers of white tissue paper rose up. Pip frowned, trying to make up her mind. Then, pawing the crackling tissue aside, she saw it. It lay folded gently around more paper and nestled in a bed of tissue below, the most beautiful dress she had ever seen.

Its color was blue, not navy, not pale, but a strong shade like a bluejay's wing. It had silver buttons down the front opening. Embroidery in red and green and white covered the collar and surrounded the buttons. Pip stepped back and pulled it from the box. It had long sleeves with embroidered cuffs and a long blue tie belt. Pip turned to her mother, hugging it to her.

"I thought you'd like it," her mother said.

"It's just what I wanted!" Pip cried. "You knew! You knew!"

"Of course I knew," her mother laughed.

White tissue paper trailed behind her as Pip leapt upstairs. She ran into her mother's bedroom at the front of the house, skinnied out of her nightgown and pulled the dress over her head. Standing barefoot before the long mirror, she looked at her reflection. The silver buttons made a line down the front. The embroidery was thick, some of it making scrolls, some flowers and some little animals. The blue was the most beautiful color she had ever seen. And there was the belt. The dress didn't hang like a little girl's. It had a belt!

"You look perfectly beautiful," said her mother from the doorway.

Pip stared at the mirror in surprise. She hadn't seen herself. It was the dress that mattered, and it was perfect.

"You must write your father and tell him your mother finally got you a dress."

Pip's spirits dived sharply. She didn't know how to tell her father about the dress or about anything. He was far away, and he never understood.

"I'll tell Radyar."

"He and Andy went back to Los Angeles."

"Will he ever come back?"

Her mother smiled. "You really did like your ride on his motorcycle, didn't you?"

Pip didn't reply. Some things her mother knew, and some things she didn't understand at all.

# ❦ 4 ❦

## The Chicken Committee

THE BLUE EMBROIDERED DRESS hung on her closet door where she could look at it. Early Monday morning Pip pulled the matching blue bloomers over her white underpants and stepped into the dress. She buttoned the silver buttons and tied the belt in front. Sitting on the edge of the wardrobe floor she pulled on white socks that came up almost to her knee and stuffed her feet into her brown sandals and buckled the straps. All the time she found it hard to force full breaths into her lungs because her stomach felt hard and rigid. It was the first day of school.

"I'll bet you're scared," Parkman jeered.

"I am not," she muttered, not trusting her voice.

"I am sort of," he said, and she was sorry she hadn't been honest.

She let her hand slide over the white bark of the sycamore tree as she passed, and its smoothness reassured her a little. Parkman led the way along the path through the oaks, his corduroy knickers going swish-swish with each step he took. When they came to the blacktopped road, he held out both arms to keep her back and looked both directions. Pip glanced back, but the house was hidden by the trees.

Parkman crossed the road and took the path again through the grove until it came to an end at another blacktopped road. The school was right there in front of them.

It was the same school where she had gone last year, but it seemed strange and new. In the middle of the playfield Parkman pointed to the Lower School where her room was and walked away. She watched him go, listening to the swishing of his corduroy knickers until he disappeared into the Upper School building. She was alone. Wondering if she should run away, she raised her hand to her mouth. The embroidery on the cuff caught her eye. She might tear her dress, playing in it all day, but there was something else, too, which reassured her. She did not know what the feeling meant, but feeling it, she crossed the playfield to the Lower School and entered her classroom.

The room was different from last year's room. It was bigger and L-shaped, and it made her feel older and more grown-up and less pressed in upon. The little yellow oak chairs were already placed in a semicircle in front of the big yellow oak chair.

From the doorway Pip saw only two people in the room. Marjorie Steadman was already there. Her pale hair was bleached even whiter than Pip remembered it, and she wore her yellow dress with the white collar and cuffs. It had buttons in back where she had to be helped and no belt. Pip noticed the line between lighter and darker where the hem had been let down. Marjorie was placing a book on each chair which gave Pip a twinge of envy. Between chairs Marjorie gave a little happy skip. The other person in the room stood behind the teacher's desk counting a stack of thick brown wood pencils. Her hair was brown and short and curled forward on her cheeks like Pip's mother's. But the teacher's hair was shingled in black like a boy's, and her crinkled-up eyes looked out from beneath a forehead covered with thick brown bangs.

"I'm Miss Sixe," she said brightly. "And who are you?"

Pip looked at her without answering.

"That's Pip dePuyster," Marjorie shrieked. "Her real name is Ann Margaret."

Pip and the teacher regarded each other steadily for half a minute.

"Do you like to be called Ann Margaret or would you rather be called Pip?"

After a full minute's thought she said, "Pip."

"Then I'll call you Pip." Miss Sixe tapped the ends of the brown wood pencils together. "What a pretty and unusual dress." Pip felt the knot inside her loosen.

"Are you new?" she asked.

Miss Sixe looked serious for a moment. "Yes, I am. I'm a little frightened."

"The first day is always the worst," Pip said.

"I think you're right," Miss Sixe smiled.

Now other girls and boys began to come through the door from the school grounds. Some of them she recognized from last year. A few she had never seen before, but it was hard to tell the ones she knew from the ones she didn't. She hadn't seen them all summer, and now they looked different. Barian Nicholson had grown taller than any of the girls. One new boy was so small and his color so gray that he looked as if he had never been outside in the sunshine. He hung back fom the others with his hands pushed into his pockets.

Miss Sixe directed them to the little semicircle of chairs in front of her chair so that they could tell each other what they had done during the summer. She wanted to get acquainted, she said.

Right away Marjorie Steadman raised her hand, pressing the inside of her elbow against her white head and flicking her hand like a little flag. She wanted to be first so much that Pip surged with disgust. Miss Sixe called on her, and Marjorie stood against Miss Sixe's chair and let Miss Sixe put her arm around her while she told about living all summer at the beach and how the sand plugged up the drain in the shower bath and the fog frosted the windows with salt until you couldn't see out.

The next turn went to Barian Nicholson because he just got up and stood next to Miss Sixe. He had taken care of his goat. It was just a little goat when he got it in June, but it grew and grew and ate his gym shoes while he went barefoot on the Fourth of July. Now it was as big as a Shetland pony and had grown long white hair. It was an Angora goat, Barian said, that was the kind with long hair.

Across the semicircle sat the small gray-colored boy. His turn approaching, his huge dark gray eyes stared straight ahead, and he held tight to the seat of his chair as if he might be thrown off. Where his right hand clutched the wood, Pip noticed that he had only three fingers. The sight gave her stomach a thump. No wonder he kept his hands in his pockets. When his turn came, the boy could only mutter his name which was Harold.

As her turn came closer, Pip's stomach hardened again and her breaths would not go down all the way. She did not want to say that she had gone to Kansas City to live with her father, and that she and Parkman had gone alone on The Golden State Train, and on the way back she had stood on the open platform of the observation car and thrown the baby doll her father had made her take onto the tracks as they came out clicking from under the train. The doll fell against the wooden tie, one leg hooked on the rail, and grew smaller with every click. She had been shocked to see how broken and helpless it looked all alone in the great space. Parkman howled with laughter, shouting, "How are you going to get it back?" And she couldn't answer, not even to say that she didn't want it back. With Miss Sixe's eyes looking steadily at her, Pip pressed her lips shut and tried to force her breath into her lungs.

"You don't have to tell us anything, if you don't want to," Miss Sixe said. Pip glared darkly. "Well, let's see, who is next? Barian told us about his goat — now —"

After that everyone told about his animal, if he had one, and about the animal of someone he knew if he didn't. Parkman's turtle, the tarantula, Mrs. Huckaby's scorpions came into Pip's mind, but she wasn't going to say anything now, chiming in like a copycat. The very idea disgusted her.

"All of you are so interested in animals," Miss Sixe said, "I wonder if we should have some here. We can learn to take care of them and watch them grow up — would you like that?"

Marjorie Steadman clapped her hands and the others cheered. A seed of suspicion sprouted in Pip's mind.

"I think we would have to have animals we can keep in a cage or a house so that we can watch them."

"Monkeys!" Barian cried out. "Monkeys live in cages."

"Does anyone know where we can get a monkey?"

But no one did. The little group fell into a sad silence.

"There's chickens," Pip said, and the class jeered until Miss Sixe said, "Chickens! What a good idea! We can easily get chickens."

Pip's spirits rose with pleasure. Everyone looked at her, the jeers changed into respect.

"Chickens would be perfect," Miss Sixe went on. "They are small. They are easy to take care of, and the lunchroom could use the eggs." She smiled at Pip. "That is a very good idea."

Pip wondered what made her think of it. She was not the least bit interested in chickens. Monkeys sounded much better. Barian gave her a dirty look, and she scowled back. He was too big to shove anymore, and anyway she would have to wait for recess to do it.

"Now where can we get our chickens?"

"Arzoomanian's Egg Ranch," Pip said quickly before anyone else could. "That's near the orange-packing plant."

"That's where I got my goat," Barian said.

"Oh, so you know Mr. Arzoomanian? Good. Now, if you'll take your chairs to the tables. Marjorie has passed out

[37]

the books, and I think the very first story is about chickens. Perhaps we will learn from that story what we need to know about taking care of our chickens when we get them."

The suspicion sprouting inside Pip blossomed.

After they had read the story, which was about a boy and a girl on a farm and how they raised chickens and cared for them and sold the eggs, Pip knew her suspicions were correct. They had fallen into Miss Sixe's trap. Worst of all, she had led the way. She looked through the book. There was not one picture of a monkey in it. If she had just gone along with Barian, they would not have been tricked.

But it was too late. On the black slate board Miss Sixe was making large white chalk letters which read

### CHICKEN COMMITTEE

and underneath she wrote another large white word

### CHAIRMAN

and turning back to the class, she mused, "Now whom should we ask to be the chairman of our chicken committee?"

Marjorie Steadman's arm flashed up and her hand snapped eagerly. Barian's head rose above all the others. Then Harold spoke up for the first time.

"Pip thought of it first," he said; and without hesitating Miss Sixe wrote after the word

### CHAIRMAN, PIP DEPUYSTER

A few minutes later everyone was on the committee. As chairman, Pip was to write to Mr. Arzoomanian and ask him to talk to them about chickens. Barian was appointed head carpenter for the chicken coop with the help of the other boys and Mr. Romero, the school caretaker. Harold, the boy with the three-fingered hand, headed the Chicken Bank which Marjorie Steadman was on. She did not head anything even if she had come early and passed out the books and had white hair.

Walking toward home on the blacktop road, Pip was not at all certain that she liked what had happened. When Marjorie Steadman's mother stopped her black Ford motorcar and offered her a ride, Pip refused. She wanted to walk and think and puzzle out what had happened, but after a few minutes she had stopped wondering about being tricked into chickens and began to think of herself as chairman of the committee. She saw herself talking with Mr. Arzoomanian and making the important decisions and telling the others what to do.

When she heard feet pounding behind her, she knew that Parkman was catching up. As he came up beside her, he snarled, "You're supposed to wait for me. Mother said so."

"I forgot," Pip said. They walked side by side without speaking. Then she said, "I have a new teacher."

"I'll bet she's dumb."

"She is not." Pip was a little surprised to hear herself defend Miss Sixe. "Is your teacher dumb?"

"She doesn't know anything. She hasn't even read *The Book of Knowledge*."

Pip had looked through all twenty volumes of *The Book of Knowledge* and Parkman had read to her lots of the stories. It seemed funny to her, too, that his teacher hadn't read it. Parkman knew all about a great many things from *The Book of Knowledge.* They walked in silence.

"There is a new boy in my room. He only has three fingers on one hand."

"It makes me sick to look at things like that."

Pip was silent. After they cut into the oak grove behind their house, she said, "We're going to raise chickens."

"Chickens! That's the dumbest thing yet. How are you going to read about chickens?"

"There's a story in our book."

Parkman snarled scornfully.

"There are some poems, too," she added which made it somewhat better. It was hard to be proud of chickens. "We're going to ask Mr. Arzoomanian to help us."

Parkman stopped so suddenly in the path in front of her that she bumped into him. "They are here," he whispered.

"Who?" asked Pip, looking around his arm.

"Those crazy people."

Voices drifted through the oaks, high voices like bees swarming and low voices like distant surf.

"Who is crazy?" Pip peered toward the open terrace. Her mother's friend, Mr. Livingstone, was seated in the sun at the edge of the porch. His tall thin figure bent at the hips where he sat on his sporting cane that had a little seat built into the handle. He wore a gray suit, and his face was hidden by the brim of his huge white Panama straw hat. Aunt Andrea and three other women in garden-party dresses and two men, one with a beard and a turban, hovered before him. "Mr. Livingstone isn't crazy," Pip said. "Is he?"

"Dad told me to stay away from them," Parkman said. "They are crazy as bedbugs. He told me so."

Parkman knew things she never guessed, and a wave of nervousness made her hesitate. At that moment Aunt Andrea saw her and called out, "Oh, Pip precious, that dress! You are beautiful, darling, come here. Parkman, where are you going? Your mother will be furious if you don't speak to her guests."

Without looking back Parkman dashed behind the garage, leaving Pip alone in the path. Mr. Livingstone moved his head, and his face emerged from the shadow of his hat. He had a trimmed gray beard and a gray moustache and a narrow pointed face and lively gray eyes. At that moment he did not look particularly crazy. When he saw Pip, he smiled, and as she came close to him, he held out his thin hand and said, "So you have come back to us, Pip. I am very glad."

"Hello, Mr. Livingstone," Pip said. She shook his hand carefully. Looking into his eyes for a trace of craziness, she wondered what it looked like.

Then Aunt Andrea embraced her and began to introduce her, "This is my niece, Ann Margaret. This is Mr. Singh, darling, and Mr. Mehta — and Miss —" this and Mrs. that until they went onto the terrace where Mrs. Livingstone hugged Pip to her warm, perfumed, cushioned flowered dress, all the while talking without a stop with the other ladies. Long embroidered dresses stirred around their ankles and their beads chinked as they talked. Once disentangled, Pip escaped inside where her mother helped Mrs. Hernandez put out sandwiches. The long table against the wall where they ate in bad weather gleamed with copper and candles.

"Oh, Pip, how was school, darling? Don't take too many sandwiches before anyone else has had some. Will you help Mrs. Hernandez, darling? You are a lamb."

"Isn't she beautiful in that dress?" cried Aunt Andrea. "I knew it was perfect."

Her mother smiled at her. "Give Mrs. Hernandez some help with the trays."

Pip stopped by the open door as she passed and looked out. Mr. Livingstone had come into the shade and was seated on a wicker settee. The two ladies and the bearded, turbaned Mr. Singh were seated cross-legged in a semicircle before him. Mr. Livingstone had closed the top of his cane and held it in one hand beside his knee, raising it and tapping the floor to emphasize what he said. When Mrs. Livingstone took the place beside him, the ladies in the embroidered dresses and beads found room on the floor, while the others drew up the wicker armchairs behind them. To Pip they looked like a teacher with his pupils.

"Mrs. Hernandez," she asked in the kitchen, "are they crazy people?"

Mrs. Hernandez rolled her black eyes toward the ceiling. "Aye-yie," she murmured.

"How can you tell?"

Mrs. Hernandez gave her a tray to carry and didn't answer. Pip looked through the door again. She could not see their craziness.

"How do you know?" she asked Mrs. Hernandez again beside the table. Mrs. Hernandez rolled her eyes and gave an imaginary beard a few strokes and disappeared into the kitchen.

So that was the sign. Then the ladies couldn't be crazy, only Mr. Livingstone and Mr. Singh. Pip watched through the window above the table. All the time Mr. Livingstone spoke, he used his long, thin hand, the one that did not hold the cane, sometimes with the palm up, sometimes with it out to his listeners, then with the fingers and thumb together like the bud of a flower. No one interrupted him. All the eyes she could see were fastened on him, and the backs of the other heads did not move. After a while there was a little burst of laughter, and Mr. Livingstone smiled and tapped his cane. Mr. Singh asked a question, and everyone stirred a little, turning from him to Mr. Livingstone again. Then Mr. Mehta said something. He was barefoot, and he had small brown feet with straight, strong toes. One lady in an embroidered dress removed her sandals and tucked her white feet underneath her hem.

From a wicker armchair her mother listened as intently as the rest. Aunt Andrea twisted a bright yellow curl in her fingers and smiled behind her hand. If anyone struck Pip as crazy, it was Aunt Andrea. You never knew what she would do next.

Then she realized that the group was silent. Mr. Livingstone tapped his cane three ringing strikes on the stone floor. "Yamaji is the great man, the great teacher," he said, and Pip heard him clearly.

"A great man, a great man," came the answering murmurs and after them a breathless hush.

"We must wait for Yamaji's decision," Mr. Livingstone went on. "In the meantime we must all pray to the gods that he will lead us."

"Hesu Creesto," whispered Mrs. Hernandez, crossing herself. "There is only one God. The rest are devils!"

In the rising murmur of voices and scraping of chairs Pip heard no more. Mrs. Hernandez hurried away so fast that it seemed she would go right out the kitchen door and leave them this time for good. Pip took two sandwiches in case she did.

# 🝮 5 🝮

## Mrs. Huckaby's House

**B**UT MRS. HERNANDEZ did not go right out the kitchen
door never to return. She was there at dinner time, and
early in the morning before Pip was wide awake, she heard
the screen door creak and bang and she knew Mrs. Hernandez
had come back in the gray button sweater and her mother's
last year's hat with fresh lima bean bread still warm from
the bakery tucked under her arm.

By the end of the week Miss Sixe and the way she did
things and the way the other children acted and even Harold with his strange hand had grown familiar. Around Pip
the world grew steady again.

Saturday morning seemed vacant and funny when it
came. Parkman didn't get out of bed but lay on his back,
holding his book, *David Goes to Baffin Land,* six inches
above his nose. Downstairs, her mother, reading a letter from
her father, fell silent over her coffee.

It occurred to Pip that she had not seen Mrs. Huckaby,
and she did not know for sure whether the scorpions were
still in her bathtub. She pulled her coaster wagon from the
garage and drew it up with the front wheels on a white
chalk mark. She inspected the mechanics of the propeller,

the struts, and the landing gear, murmuring to herself. When all was ready and in order, she took her seat in the wagon bed and called to the contact as she pulled out the wooden blocks. The wagon glided down the driveway to the road with enough momentum to cross the hump in the center and, with a few pushes from her extended foot, climb part way up the drive opposite.

The driveway was much steeper than her own. It went almost straight up the same hill which she skirted to go to the village. When the wagon came to a stop, she marked the place in chalk and pulled it the rest of the way uphill to an undernourished orange tree where she left it in the scrawny shade.

Other than the parched orange tree there were no trees near the house. Even the dry grass was scarce, and a fine brown dust settled over the walk and the doorsteps. The low white house exposed to the sun gave the feeling of not being finished, although Pip had never seen anyone working on it. It was more as if not all of it had been thought of yet. Pip tapped on the blue screen door which rattled loosely on its hinges and waited.

"Who's there?" came a voice several rooms away.

"It's me, Mrs. Huckaby."

"Oh, come on in, I'm in here, I've been looking for you."

Inside the screen Pip walked around a heap of dirty laundry lying on the floor. The kitchen table was covered with boxes and cans and jars of various sizes and shapes, and the counters were cluttered with more. The sink was piled

[46]

with dishes and a gigantic white cat crouched on its edge, catching the drip from the faucet on a white forepaw.

"Hello, Kellogg," Pip said. The cat stared at her with oval glassy green eyes. She went through another room which looked like a storage place for flowerpots and found Mrs. Huckaby kneeling on the bathroom floor and resting her elbows on the rim of the tub.

"Three of them today," said Mrs. Huckaby. "I was afraid something had happened to one of them. I haven't seen more than two for a week."

Crawling through the dust that had sifted onto the bottom of the tub were three small scorpions. They were dust color themselves and looked like walking shrimp. Their tails curled up. Their bodies were plated with a protective shell and feelers waved about in front as if they searched the air for messages.

"Parkman says the little ones are the really bad ones," Pip said.

"Is that right? How does he know?" Mrs. Huckaby sat back on her heels.

"He has a book called *Poisonous Livers of Mountain and Desert.*"

"And it says that about the small ones? I should think the big ones would be more poisonous."

"Maybe his book is wrong," Pip said, because it didn't sound reasonable.

"Some scientist probably wrote it, and he knows," said Mrs. Huckaby. "These are the little ones all right."

[47]

"Did you find out how they get into the drainpipe?"

Mrs. Huckaby shook her head. "If there's a break in the drainpipe, I wouldn't know. I haven't used this tub for a year, not since I first found them in here."

One scorpion dropped out of sight down the drain while the other two scuttled through the dust, waving their feelers.

"The nut loaf you sent over was awfully good, Mrs. Huckaby. Mother wants the recipe. Parkman wouldn't eat it because of the black gravy. He doesn't like black food. But everybody else liked it. Especially Radyar."

"Radyar? Have I heard of him before?"

"He's Aunt Andy's new friend. Parkman says he wants to marry somebody with lots of money."

"Your Aunt Andy maybe?"

"My mother doesn't think so."

"Maybe your mother then?"

Pip lifted her hand to her mouth, staring at Mrs. Huckaby. "Do you think he likes my mother?"

"Well, I don't know, Pip. I was just examining the possibilities. Nothing has happened to that flour mill in Kansas City, has it?"

Pip shook her head, seeing the long white row of silos four stories high and almost a mile long with PARKMAN MILLS in black letters one on each silo. "I saw it last summer."

"Well, your mother is very smart. She won't be taken in. Does this Radyar do anything?"

"He tells your fortune from the stars. I forget what that's called."

"An astrologer. Really?" Mrs. Huckaby snapped her fingers. "He writes Madame Solar's column. That's where I heard his name."

"He's going to do my —" She had forgotten the word.

"Horoscope?"

Pip nodded. "He does them for lots of people, movie stars even."

"How much?" asked Mrs. Huckaby. It hadn't occurred to Pip that Radyar made money doing horoscopes. She was a little offended at the idea.

"He didn't say, Mrs. Huckaby. I don't think he charges."

"It's that or marry somebody with money," said Mrs. Huckaby. The scorpions had disappeared into the drain. "Well, I have some new crackers, Pip. I'd like to know what you think of them."

Mrs. Huckaby got up and led the way to the kitchen. She was not a very tall woman or very big around, but she wasn't skinny, either. She was round but not cushiony like Mrs. Livingstone, and she wore a man's shirt and a peasant skirt and a pair of high black boy's gym shoes like Pip's. Tied around her waist was a large white butcher's apron. She pushed things aside on the kitchen table, making a place for Pip, and put a thick white plate in front of her chair.

Kellogg took the third chair. His pink ears and nose and oval green eyes set in his great white ruff just showed above the table. In front of him Mrs. Huckaby set another white plate and poured out cream so yellow and thick it had lumps.

"Now where the deuce is that new box?" Looking at wrappers and labels, she rummaged over the tabletop.

"Maybe it's on the sink," Pip said. "What are they called?"

Mrs. Huckaby scanned the counter. "They are called —" Then she leaned under the table and pushed some boxes aside. "Here they are." She brought up an already opened box. "Vegetized crackers," she read from the label. "Like lima bean bread, Pip, made from vegetable flour."

"Parkman says flour is always from vegetables."

"Well, not always," said Mrs. Huckaby, "but mostly the vegetable is wheat, one of the grains, and this flour is from other vegetables, mostly beans of one kind or another."

"Does that make them better for you?"

"Well, they're very healthy," said Mrs. Huckaby putting two on her plate. Pip tasted one, considering as she chewed it.

"It's awfully dry, Mrs. Huckaby. It's good, but —"

Pawing over the table, Mrs. Huckaby found a jar and opened it. She spread a knifeful of the contents over Pip's second cracker. "Try this — malted nuts."

Pip took up the second cracker and bit into it, while Mrs. Huckaby watched her closely. "Do you think they'll sell, Pip?"

After chewing and considering and swallowing, Pip said, "That makes it much better. Malted nuts are delicious. May I have some more?"

[50]

"Certainly." Leaning across the table, Mrs. Huckaby snapped Kellogg on the forehead and said, "No paws on the table." Kellogg sat back and blinked contritely. The yellow cream was gone. "Well, that's the way I'll sell them then, one box vegetized crackers and one jar malted nuts. They go together, I'll tell them."

"And they'll be even healthier, won't they?"

Mrs. Huckaby nodded. "Two are always better than one."

Nibbling her second cracker, Pip thought of Harold and wondered if the right food could put a finger on his hand, but Mrs. Huckaby's face saddened when she heard the story and she shook her head. "There are limits, Pip, there are limits. Even health food can't do everything."

"I wonder if they would make Mr. Zick feel better?"

"What's the matter with him?" asked Mrs. Huckaby.

"He can hardly breathe. I think it's asthma sometimes, and sometimes it's hay fever. His office is full of steam all the time. He has a tea kettle on a little stove, and he puts eucalyptus oil in the water. Even then he can hardly breathe."

"Eats all the wrong things no doubt," muttered Mrs. Huckaby. "Meat and store bread and whatnot, couldn't be worse. Who'd you say can't breathe?"

"Mr. Zick. He runs the Valley Paramount. He lives in his office right there. That's where the steam is."

"By himself?" asked Mrs. Huckaby.

"I don't think anyone else could stand the steam, Mrs. Huckaby," Pip said.

"I suppose not. All alone, you say? He's not married?"

"I don't think so." She had never wondered if there was a Mrs. Zick. She had never seen or heard of her.

"Probably eats in restaurants, cheap cafés," Mrs. Huckaby looked vacantly across the room. "Poor man. Couldn't be worse, couldn't be worse. I'll tell you, Pip, while you're copying down this nut loaf receipt for your mother, I'll put up a packet for Mr. Zick. Just two or three things, a gift, no charge, but I'll put in my list of health foods and a note that I'll be coming around to see him. I think I can help him feel a lot better. I know I can. When are you going to see him?"

"I was going there when I left here," Pip said. "I have to pick up Parkman's collection."

Pushing her jars and boxes farther aside, Mrs. Huckaby put a large pad of yellow paper in front of Pip and gave her a pencil and a small white card which read "Nut Loaf Receipt." When Mrs. Huckaby said receipt, she meant recipe. Pip didn't know why she used such a funny word.

While Pip copied it carefully, Mrs. Huckaby put jars and packages into one box and tied it with string and wrote YAMAJI on the lid. Then she packed a box of crackers, a jar of malted nuts, and two small jars of something else in another empty brown carton. On this she wrote, A GIFT FOR MR. ZICK.

When Pip had copied the recipe, she tore the sheet off the yellow pad, folded it, and put it into her coveralls pocket. She said good-bye to Kellogg, who had gone back to the sink to catch the drip on his paw, and went out. Mrs. Huckaby followed her with the box.

The driveway was so steep that Mrs. Huckaby got around in front of the wagon and held it back while Pip got in. Pip thanked her for the vegetized crackers and malted nuts, and when she was settled sitting back on both feet, she signaled to Mrs. Huckaby who let go and jumped out of the way. Pip sailed down the driveway faster and faster. At the bottom she took the turn in a wide arc to keep all four wheels on the road. The wagon continued down the blacktop, around the bend and with only three or four pushes made it to the top of the shoulder of Mrs. Huckaby's hill. From there she coasted, steering carefully with the tongue as the joystick, into the main street of the village.

Because it was right in the village she did not mark the road where the wagon stopped. There was a telephone pole opposite her, and she made a small inconspicuous *x* on its greasy brown surface just above the clump of grass growing around its base. From there she pulled the wagon around the corner by the post office, past the small shops and under Mr. Zick's marquee.

The pictures had changed in the display windows. Clara Bow, the It girl, and Tom Mix on his rearing horse had gone. Rin Tin Tin leaping over the prison wall was Now. Next was Jean Harlow who had white hair and black butterfly lips and practically no eyebrows at all. Coming Soon would be Charlie Chaplin in *The Circus.* The window for Coming Attractions was empty, and the glass hung open. Mr. Zick's office door swung in, and he appeared in a cloud of steam. Little beads of it stood out on his cheeks.

"Well, if it isn't Pip. Where've you been? How's tricks?"

"I haven't been able to come because I'm chairman of the chicken committee, Mr. Zick."

"The what?" He almost swallowed the thumbtack he held between his lips.

"At school we're going to have chickens. I'm chairman of the committee."

Mr. Zick went back to thumbtacking the pictures in the display window. "So this year it's chickens, is it? Last year what was it? Anthills, red ants and black ants. So it's chickens. Ants are better, Pip. They don't make a mess."

Pip hadn't thought of the mess before. Miss Sixe hadn't mentioned it, and neither had the story in their reader. Although it described cleaning the coop, it didn't say why. She should have known; she had been to the zoo. Thoughtfully, she rubbed one ankle with the toe of her other gym shoe.

"Did you know White Leghorn chickens lay more eggs than Rhode Island Reds?"

"This Rhode Island Red I never heard of, nor a White Leghorn, either."

"Do you think we should get White Leghorns, Mr. Zick? They aren't half as beautiful as Rhode Island Reds."

"It depends what you want, little Pip, more to eat or more to look at," said Mr. Zick, closing the glass and turning the key in the little round lock. "What have you got in the box, chicken feed?"

Pip had forgotten about Mrs. Huckaby's package. "Oh, no, it's for you. You know Mrs. Huckaby, the health food lady?"

"The what?" said Mr. Zick. "I've never had the pleasure."

"I told her about your asthma, and she sent some things for you to eat. They'll make you feel a lot better."

Mr. Zick took the box. "I'll try anything — even this malted nuts. I could feel better, but I could feel worse. You want Parkman's collection?"

Between them they carried a stack of the shiny black and white show pictures from Mr. Zick's office. It was like going in and out of a cloud. Once she was used to it, Pip didn't mind the steam and the smell of the eucalpytus oil which was pungent and strong like the eucalyptus groves in the rain. When they had stowed them away in the back of the wagon, Pip got in. Mr. Zick pulled out the wooden blocks from the wheels, stood back, and they exchanged salutes as she coasted past him.

When she looked back at the corner to wave, Mr. Zick didn't notice her. He was reading Mrs. Huckaby's note.

# ⊠ 6 ⊠

## Letters

PIP GAVE GREAT THOUGHT to the letter to Mr. Arzoomanian before she sat down to write on her lined tablet.
For one thing, there was Mr. Arzoomanian's name, the
longest word she knew of, and she had to spell it right. She
didn't like it when anyone spelled dePuyster wrong or pro-
nounced it de-pooey-ster instead of dePiester the way it should
be. It took her till the end of the week to get everything in
Mr. Arzoomanian's letter right, what she said and how she
said it, and writing it without erasing a lot.

That Saturday her mother lay in the darkened bedroom
at the head of the stairs. The back of one hand rested on her
forehead, and the other hand held a letter on her stomach.
Pip crossed the bare floor from the doorway to the bed. Her
gym shoes made little squeaks at each step. She stood beside
the bed and looked at the letter. It was from her father. She
recognized his handwriting, although she couldn't read it
because the letters ran together. After a minute or two her
mother smiled a little and turned her head toward Pip.

"I can hear you breathing, darling," she murmured.

"Is it bad?"

Her mother groaned and turned away, the letter rustling as she moved.

"It is the worst. It makes me sick to my stomach, and that has never happened before." She sighed. "Mrs. Huckaby is coming as soon as she can. She was so much help last time."

"Do you want anything?" Pip asked.

"No, no, dear." The letter fluttered from her hand as she reached out to pat Pip's arm. "It's only a headache, don't worry."

Pip squeaked to the window and opened one shutter a crack. Mrs. Huckaby was crossing the road below, carrying a large basket over one arm and followed by Kellogg who held his great white tail upright like a skunk's. Mrs. Huckaby strode up the driveway, crossed to the front door, and walked in without knocking. In a second, Pip heard her springing up the stairs, every so often two steps at a time, her gym shoes squeaking. She stood in the doorway a moment, looked at her mother, at Pip, and went straight to the love seat between the windows.

"So it's pretty bad, Dorrit?" she said.

"My worst."

Pip moved behind the love seat to examine the contents of the basket. It was full of metal plates and wires heaped on a black box with dials on it. Mrs. Huckaby pulled the plates out, one in one hand, one in the other, the black wires dangling, and laid them on the back of the little sofa. Pip thought of the tarantula with its long hairy legs.

Mrs. Huckaby laid one metal plate on her mother's forehead. "All right, that's one," she said briskly. The long wire dangled over the edge of the bed. The second plate she strapped around her mother's upper arm, the third on her other arm, the black wire lying on her mother's chest. Mrs. Huckaby plugged the wires into sockets in the black box and handed the cord from the box to Pip. "Can you find the socket?" she asked. Pip ducked behind the love seat and screwed the plug into the electrical outlet.

Mrs. Huckaby checked the plates on her mother's head and arms again, inspected the wires and the box. "I have two extra pieces," she said. "I can give you a treatment, too, Pip. Lie down right here."

"I'm not sick," Pip said.

"It doesn't matter," said Mrs. Huckaby. "It'll do you a lot of good."

Pip lay down on the love seat and crossed her ankles. Mrs. Huckaby tied the plates to her upper arms and plugged in the wires. "Are we all set?" she asked. "Ready now. You must lie still for half an hour." Then she flipped a switch on the black box and adjusted the dials.

The dim room grew heavy with silence. Pip listened intently. The machine made no noise. It did not purr or click or sizzle like the two-box radio behind the sofa downstairs. The plates were cold at first, but now they gave no sensation whatsoever. She didn't feel any electrical shock like the one she got when she and Parkman had put their fingers in the wall socket to see what would happen. There was a terrible itch in her armpit. She didn't dare move one arm to scratch it. Kellogg came in the room and sat on her stomach, staring at her with his oval eyes black as raisins in the darkness. His white hair tickled her nose. When he began to make bread with his claws on her chest, Mrs. Huckaby picked him up and scolded him.

Half an hour was a long time. Parkman came in and looked and went out, taking Kellogg with him. Mrs. Huckaby moved about, checking the metal plates and the wires and the dials. "Better?" she asked her mother.

"Yes, I think so," her mother whispered.

The box made a click. "Time's up!" Mrs. Huckaby exclaimed. She flicked the switch and unscrewed the plug at the wall. When she had loosened all the wires, she began to remove the black plates.

"I can't believe it," said her mother, "but do you know, my headache is gone."

"Of course, it is," said Mrs. Huckaby. "And how do you feel, Pip?"

"Fine," Pip said. She had felt fine to begin with. She laid her metal plates in the basket on top of the box.

"I really do feel much, much better. Pip, run down and ask Mrs. Hernandez to bring us some coffee."

"Wait a minute," said Mrs. Huckaby. "I picked up some fresh lima bean buns while I was out. If Mrs. Hernandez will just pop them in the oven a minute while she makes the coffee —"

Pip took the white paper package and went downstairs. She could discover nothing new or curious in what she felt.

Parkman grabbed her by the arm at the foot of the stairs. "What does it do to you?" he whispered. Pip pulled away without answering. "I'll bet nothing," he jeered.

"Humph," Pip said and went into the kitchen.

For once Parkman walked beside her all the way to the Valley Paramount that afternoon, trying to get her to tell him what Mrs. Huckaby's machinery did. The more he was dying to know the more she was determined not to tell. "It doesn't do anything, that's why you won't tell me," he said.

"It cured Mother's headache," she said. Parkman had nothing to say to that.

The crowd under the marquee was already huge. Harold stood against the big colored poster on the wall, his hands in his pockets, all alone. He watched Pip as she and Parkman came closer, his gray eyes wide and lifeless in his pale gray face. He made Pip so nervous with pity and distaste that she marched past him without speaking. Marjorie Steadman squealed at her from her post at the inside door, shrieking and waving her arm as if she wanted to give an answer. Pip ignored her, too, following Parkman in line for the ticket window.

The eucalyptus-scented steam filled the ticket booth and billowed out through the little half-moon window at the bottom of the glass. Inside Mr. Zick took Parkman's fifteen cents and pushed a yellow ticket through the hole.

"Hello, Mr. Zick," Pip laid a dime and one nickel from her coveralls pocket on the ledge.

"How's tricks, Pip? You'll like this show, Pip. Rin Tin Tin belongs to some good ranchers and he finds the bad cowboys — well, I won't tell you, or you'll keep your money."

"I wouldn't keep it for anything, Mr. Zick." She put her mouth close to the window so that Parkman couldn't hear. "Did you find out about *Wings*, Mr. Zick?"

He shook his head. "Not yet, Pip, not yet. Maybe soon I'll know."

The eucalyptus mist swirled about her head. She took her yellow ticket and followed Parkman. Marjorie Steadman was giggling and going up and down on her toes like a ballet dancer in front of Barian Nicholson, which disgusted Pip. She was a big show-off all the time. "Don't you ever wear a dress on Saturday, Pip dePuyster?" she yelled over everybody's head. "I bet you only have one."

Pip gathered herself like a battering ram. Head down, she went for Marjorie Steadman's stomach, but before she hit, Mr. Zick opened the doors and she shot through without running into anybody. Marjorie danced ahead across the carpet to the inner doors.

The sound inside the theater was almost as solid as a wall. Thumps and clunks and scrapings accompanied the high shrieking voices. At first Pip stopped at the head of the aisle. She could not get through the barrier, but someone behind pushed her into it. She went down a few rows halfway to the front and found a seat. The noise wasn't so bad once she sat down. She looked around for Parkman but couldn't find him. Barian Nicholson and another boy fell on the floor wrestling right beside her. When Barian got up, he grabbed the seat next to her. The other boy sat in his lap. Barian pounded him in the ribs, and he slid into the farther seat. Barian had a little white paper sack in his hand and when he opened it, she could smell green candy mint leaves. "Want one?" he asked. She put her hand in and took one, but she didn't speak to him. Anyone dumb enough to act like that in the movies didn't deserve to be spoken to.

Then the theater darkened, the voices shrieked louder and higher. Pip put her hands over her ears, carefully keeping her lips closed to trap all the mint exploding in her mouth. The black screen flickered with streaks of white, and the screams rose higher until the screen exploded with light. RIN TIN TIN said the big black letters. The shrieking increased. IN. THE NIGHT CRY. Pressing her hands to her ears, Pip put her head down on her knees. Whistles pierced the shrieking. Yelling and jumping and clapping, Barian forgot about the little white bag. Pip saw it slide across his corduroy knickers and plop right side up beneath her foot. She reached down and took another green mint leaf. Barian was too dumb to notice.

Afterwards when Parkman demanded to know what part she liked best, she could only remember one scene. The bad men had gone through a trapdoor in the floor of the ranch house, and other bad people had covered the trapdoor with a rug. When the good men and Rinty came into the room, Rinty sniffed around the room. Then he began to growl and pull at the rug. The bad people stood on it, but the good men with Rinty made them step aside. Rinty pulled the rug away, and there was the trapdoor. The screaming reached such a pitch that Pip covered her ears and ducked her head again. The little white sack was empty.

"Did you really like that best?" Parkman said scornfully. "That's not the best part."

"Barian Nicholson was crawling around all the time trying to find his candy. I could hardly watch," she said. The smell of the mint in her mouth and the easiness of taking more whenever she wanted a piece and the thought of stuffing the bag in her pocket had distracted her the whole time. All the way home she listened to Parkman tell the movie's story from beginning to end. She could never have done it, and she was dissatisfied with herself.

Where the road curved around the hill, they left it and walked through the oak grove toward the front of their house.

As Pip reached for the doorknob, the door opened and her mother stepped out. Behind her was Radyar, and this time he wasn't wearing riding pants and puttees but white trousers and a deep blue jacket with a red scarf tucked inside the collar. Where, Pip wondered, was Aunt Andrea? Parkman spoke in a sort of growl and pushed past them into the house.

"Parkman, will you please be polite?" her mother said. Radyar stopped still and held out his hand to Pip. He smiled with all his white teeth. "Ah, Pip!" he exclaimed.

"Hello," she said, suddenly uncertain.

"How was the movie, darling?" Her mother looked particularly pretty in a purple-red bumpy-knitted suit.

"All right," Pip said. "Are you going someplace?"

"We're going to the Livingstones'. Mrs. Hernandez will be here until I get home. Write your father, dearest, you said you would."

Pip watched them get on the motorcycle, her mother tucking herself into the sidecar but not putting on the helmet, Radyar mounting the machine, stepping down hard on the starter three or four times before the motor caught. He wheeled the cycle around, put on his helmet and adjusted the goggles, and raised his arm to Pip. She lifted her hand in reply. Then they roared down the drive and went out of sight behind the bramble hedge. She listened to the sound of the motor until it faded away.

When the drive was empty, she went inside. Parkman was not in the living room. He must have gone right upstairs. She sat down on the painted black chair in front of the painted black desk and thought for a few minutes. She wondered where her Aunt Andrea was and whether she had a newer friend than Radyar, now that Radyar seemed to be her mother's friend. Wondering and trying to think, she studied the photograph above the desk. It was tinted with browns and oranges and showed a noble Indian on his horse with his arms spread wide behind him. He did not look like the Indians she saw in the movies who were fierce and angry or the ones in colorful clothes she had seen seated under the arcade of the Albuquerque railroad station where she had bought a turquoise ring for a dollar. This Indian wore only a tiny apron, and he had muscles on his chest like plates. She wondered what tribe this Indian belonged to and if he was the only one left. Then she fell to thinking of her father far away in Kansas City, and she knew that her letter should be right, like her letter to Mr. Arzoomanian after Miss Sixe had corrected it.

There was an inkstand on the desk with a bottle of washable blue ink. Lying in a groove was a pen with a silver point. She had never used the pen before, and it felt different, thick where her fingers held it and slimmer toward the top. She dipped the point in the ink bottle and began to write:

*Dear Daddy*
*I am fine. How are you?*
*We are studying chickens in school.*
*I went to the movies today.*
*Parkman went too.*
*We saw Rin Tin Tin in The Night Cry.*
*Today is Saturday.*
*Mother is out with*

She wondered how to spell Radyar. She didn't know. Astrologer was impossible. She thought and then wrote carefully

*a man.*

*Love,*

*Pip*

When she had finished, she didn't like the looks of ink very well. There were too many spots. But, on the other hand, she did like it. Her mother used ink. Next time she would try not to get so much on her hands.

# ▨ 7 ▨

## Chicken Help

MR. ARZOOMANIAN was a big, brown-faced man with a huge gray moustache and gray hair that looked as if he never combed it. When he came to the school, he wore a blue work shirt and blue and white striped overalls that pulled across his belly. In a cardboard box he had a dozen little yellow chicks. They were White Leghorns, he said, or they would be when they grew up and got white feathers. They would be good layers. He took one out of the box and held it in his big brown palm. The children pressed forward to see. The baby chick peeped twice and on the callus at the base of his little finger made a dropping.

"That's a chicken for you," said Mr. Arzoomanian with a roar of laughter. He wiped his hand on the back of his overalls leg. The boys snickered. Pip's opinion of chickens, already low, sank further.

"Rhode Island Reds have colored feathers," she said. The class stirred with interest.

"What do you care how they look?" Mr. Arzoomanian asked. "These'll get you more eggs. A chicken is a machine for making eggs." He guffawed again.

That anything was just a machine for doing something shocked Pip, and she spoke up, "We haven't decided yet."

"I think we have to take Mr. Arzoomanian's advice," Miss Sixe said.

"But we don't have a place for them." If she had time, she could persuade or bully the class, she was certain.

"A couple of days they can stay in the box," said Mr. Arzoomanian. "Then Barian here and Mr. Romero and the boys can get the coop built. You can add the hen house later, if you want it, before the nights get cold."

"But I'm chairman!" Pip exclaimed. The whole class laughed which infuriated her. They were taking away her job. It was not at all funny, and she hated feeling ridiculous.

But the matter was settled. Mr. Arzoomanian met with Barian and the other boys and Mr. Romero to plan the coop.

Pip watched them chattering and planning. She had been chairman of nothing. Miss Sixe and Mr. Arzoomanian and Mr. Romero, they ran it all, and none of the others cared or even noticed.

"I like Rhode Island Reds best, too," Marjorie Steadman said, but Pip was too hurt to let anyone take her side and she glared at Marjorie.

Seated at a round table, Harold, who was chairman of the chicken bank, tried to figure out how much it cost for twelve chicks if one chick cost twenty-five cents. The way he held the thick brown pencil in his three-fingered hand looked funny, but he had the answer faster than anybody else in the chicken bank. It came to three dollars, he said. There was a shoe box marked BANK where they had put nickels and dimes. Now he went to it and counted out three dollars. Marjorie who was a member of the banking committee checked Harold's figures, but Harold had paid Mr. Arzoomanian and he was gone before Marjorie had the answer. That was the way to be a chairman, Pip thought, be faster than everybody else.

Barian and Mr. Romero and the other boys worked for two days putting the chicken coop together. On the second day the others wandered away or found something else to do after recess until only Barian and Mr. Romero remained. Pip found a hammer lying in the grass, and Mr. Romero showed her how to pound staples into the posts. He held the chicken wire and Barian held the staple over the wire while she thumped it two and three times with the hammer. The yellow lumber, warm in the sun, smelled freshly cut.

Barian climbed to the top and sat on the crosspiece and tore his knickers getting down. After that Pip was very careful and held her dress back when she stood on the barrel to hammer. Mr. Romero smiled and nodded and said, "Like this, miss" to her and "Careful, young man" to Barian. Later when he opened his lunch box in the shade of an oak, they sat with him and took little sips of milky coffee from his Thermos bottle. He gave them a taste of his beans and sausage folded in tortillas, but Pip didn't like it much. The sausage burned her tongue, and the rest was mushy and tasteless.

When Marjorie came out for lunch, she did her pedaling-with-wings ballet exercise in front of them and giggled and tossed her white hair.

"Hair like an angel," Mr. Romero murmured, smiling. Pip was so disgusted she was ready to butt the big show-off in the stomach, but Mr. Romero's admiration stopped her. Barian was looking at Marjorie's hair as if he had never seen it before. Patting her own moist curling mop Pip was suddenly envious.

Once they were in the coop, the little chicks grew rapidly. Real feathers began to appear among the yellow fluff. Soon they were half-size. Every week a new list of names appeared on the classroom blackboard. Under CHICKEN HELP were the chores which needed to be done every day: clean the water trough; fill it with fresh water; fill the grain dishes; mix the mash; and, the last, clean the coop.

In the few weeks they had the chicks, Pip came to hate every chore. Filling the grain bowls was all right, but it was nothing. The water trough grew a scum all over the insides, and this had to be scrubbed away. It felt cold and slimy and smelled stagnant and rotten. As soon as the water was added to the meal for the mash, the odor rose in a great cloud almost too thick to breathe. But cleaning the coop was the worst. The foul odor of the droppings rose on the dust as she raked the ground inside the coop, and she could not take a deep breath. Chickens made a mess, Mr. Zick was right. And, besides, they were dumb. They had stupid little eyes and scrawny ugly necks and they picked their way through their own filth, plopped droppings in their own water, and pecked each other for no reason.

The second time her turn came up to clean the coop, she took the rake from Mr. Romero's workroom and set to work. She tried to hold her breath, but she could not do it long enough. Her feet dragged. The others finished their chores, and she was still working. She hated being last. The class gathered under the oak to do silent reading while they waited for her. "Hurry up," Miss Sixe called. Pip turned her back to the group and took two more swipes at the bare ground. Then she propped the rake against the wire. She would not do it. She would not be chicken help ever again.

The class reading under the oaks infuriated her. They had no discrimination. They would do anything they were told. The rake clattered to the ground from where she had propped it. Miss Sixe looked up.

"Pip dePuyster, where are you going?" she called out.

"Home," Pip muttered, walking fast.

"Pip, come back here. School is not out."

She walked faster without looking back. She heard Miss Sixe coming. Before Miss Sixe could grip her arm tightly, Pip jerked away and began to run.

"Pip dePuyster, I want to talk with you," came the voice. Then farther and farther away, "I want to talk to you . . . I want to talk to you . . ."

Pip darted across the road and into the grove of oaks. She didn't stop running until she came to the next crossing. Her heart pounded and she was out of breath. She looked back. The path was empty. She crossed the road and walked slowly, taking deep breaths. She could see in every direction through the great oaks. No one followed her.

She walked slowly toward her house. It came to her that school was not over yet and her mother would wonder why she was home. She moved up behind the sycamore and studied the house. People were there. She saw Mr. Livingstone through the open door and the women who wore embroidered dresses. She saw her mother who was wearing a white dress with embroidery like her own blue one. Moving quickly, she caught hold of the sycamore's lower branch, placed one foot against the tree and ran up the trunk, crossed to the horizontal limb and slid into the hollow. Only the top of her head showed.

She sat there thinking for some time. Her first thought was to kick Miss Sixe when she tried to make her clean the coop next time, but she knew she couldn't. After a long time she thought of Harold. He would do it for her. He didn't have any friends. But it was a dirty trick. She was turning this plan over in her mind when she saw a brown hand move up the trunk of the white sycamore. She sat up straighter and looked out. A man in white clothes stood by the tree, and just as she moved, he turned and noticed her.

For a moment they looked at each other in surprise. The man had a dark face and a long thin nose and very large dark eyes. His hair was black and thick and his eyebrows were black and almost met in the middle. After a moment he smiled very gently. "Hello," he said.

"Hello." Pip held out her hand over the side of the limb.

He took her hand and smiled. "I envy you being able to hide in this beautiful tree."

"I'm not hiding," Pip said. "I was, but I'm not anymore. I was just thinking."

The man nodded. "It is a good place to think, when something is troubling. I find a tree a great help."

"Do you have some trouble?" Pip found it hard to believe.

The man nodded. "Yes, I am troubled now. That is why I came out here. Do you have some troubles?"

He was as brown as Mr. Romero and so very gentle and quiet that she trusted him without thinking. She told him about being chicken help, how she hated chickens. They were so dumb and so dirty that she couldn't breathe when she raked the chicken coop, and she wouldn't do it. While she told the story, her heart began pounding again. "They are trying to make me," she cried, "and I won't do it. I won't!"

The man listened without moving, one brown hand resting on the great limb. When she finished, he waited until she had caught her breath again.

"Have you told them how you feel?" he asked.

She was silent. She had run away without telling anyone why. She imagined herself telling Miss Sixe what she had just told the brown-faced man, and she saw Miss Sixe listening, but what Miss Sixe did after she listened wasn't clear.

"They are trying to make me do something, too," the man said with a little smile.

"Clean a chicken coop?"

"No, no," he laughed. "Something else they want me to do, something they want me to be for them."

"Who?"

"Some very strong people whom I love very much. They are in this house now."

"Is that why you came out to my tree?"

"So this is your tree. It is very beautiful and unusual."

"It's a good thinking place," Pip said.

The man, smiling, held out his brown hand. "My name is Yamaji."

"Hello, Mr. Yamaji." She took his hand and searched his face. "Are you a great man?" She wanted to remember forever what a great man looked like.

Yamaji smiled. "That is one of the things they want me to be."

"It isn't as bad as being chicken help," Pip said.

Laughing, Yamaji said, "I think they want me to be the chicken."

"I wouldn't be a chicken for anything," Pip exclaimed.

"I think that is my answer," Yamaji said. He turned back toward the house.

Watching him go, Pip saw clearly her own course. She would not be a chicken, either, doing without thinking what they wanted her to do. Harold would do her assignments for her. All she had to do was to tell him that if he did, she would be his friend.

# ◙ 8 ◙

## Harold

B EFORE SHE NOTICED, Parkman had stopped in the path
ahead of her, and she bumped into him.

"Watch what you're doing," Parkman said.

"What?"

"You're still asleep."

Pip was too confused to answer. Walking along the path
to school behind Parkman, she was thinking about Harold.
Last night, secretly, she had picked up the black upright
telephone and taken the earpiece from the hook and whispered Harold's telephone number to the operator. She had
to repeat it because the operator couldn't hear her. She
whispered so that her mother or Parkman wouldn't listen
and ask questions. When she asked to speak to Harold, his
mother had to ask, who? But Harold heard her. His voice
went high and thin in surprise, and he answered eagerly
that he would meet her before school at the chicken coop.
He didn't even ask why, and she knew she would have her
way.

This morning she was nervous and not so sure and fear-
ful that she would be found out. Crashing into Parkman

increased her confusion. She was surprised to see the white school building directly ahead across the road.

Parkman walked off toward the Upper School, and Pip hesitated in the middle of the playfield, thinking which way to take to the chicken coop. Circling around the Lower School she avoided passing her classroom where Miss Sixe might be. Mr. Romero's workroom was open. When she peeked in, he was not there. She took down the rake and went around behind the chicken coop where the shrubbery was thickest. There she waited and not for long. In a few minutes Harold rounded the corner of the building, out of breath from running.

"Psst! Harold!"

He stopped to listen, stuffing his three-fingered hand into his pocket.

"Harold, come here."

Then he saw her and pushed between the shrubs to join her. They looked at each other for a few moments, but there was no time to waste, and Pip asked, "Do you want me to be your friend?"

Harold looked at her without speaking. Pip mastered a little bubble of anger in her. "Harold, I'll be your friend, if you'll be my friend."

His gray-black eyes glistened. "I'm your friend, Pip."

"All right," Pip said impatiently. "We're friends." She tried to think of how to say what she wanted to say next.

"Real friends?" Harold asked.

"Real friends — real friends do things for each other. Harold, will you do something for me?" He nodded. "Harold, will you clean the chicken coop? I have — I can't — I have trouble breathing when I rake the dirt."

"Okay," Harold said. He took the rake from her hand, went around the coop to the gate and went inside where he began to hum as he raked. Pip squatted in the bushes, hoping no one saw her, and watched him scratch the ground with the rake. She wished he'd hurry.

Harold had trouble with the rake. The handle was too long and his three-fingered hand made an awkward grip, but he raked the entire coop. All the time he hummed softly to himself. When he finished and there was a pile of chicken droppings and dust by the gate, Pip came out of the bushes, hung up the rake, and the two of them sat down on Mr. Romero's bench. Soon after Barian came to mix the mash, and Marjorie Steadman had to clean and refill the water pans. Pip wished Harold wouldn't sit so close to her, and she gave him a hump with her shoulder.

"Are we only going to be friends before anybody comes?" he asked.

Pip was silent. It was not fair just to be friends part of the time, the time when he did what she wanted him to do. After thinking a few minutes, she said, "We're friends all the time." Then she had to let him kind of lean against her arm, even though she didn't like it.

The next morning Pip and Harold met early so that the chicken coop was raked before anyone else arrived. They were just sitting quietly side by side on the bench when Barian and Marjorie Steadman came. The following morning Pip waited and waited in the bushes, chewing her lips and frowning, until Harold appeared at a high run around the corner of the building. He was wet and puffing, but still he took the rake and hurried into the coop while Pip hissed at him angrily. At that moment Marjorie Steadman appeared.

"Harold Hoffer!" she shrieked, "you're not supposed to rake. You can't. That's Pip's job." No sooner had she spoken than she spotted Pip squatting in the bushes. "Pip dePuyster! I'm going to tell! I'm going to tell Miss Sixe. You're making Harold work."

At that Pip shot out of the shrubs and hit Marjorie Steadman headfirst, right in the stomach. Marjorie tumbled over backwards, her white hair flying all directions and her mouth falling open in a soundless shriek.

"You tell, and I'll do it again," Pip snarled as she stood over her. Marjorie scrambled to her feet and backed away holding out her yellow dress. "Now I'm all dirty. I'm going to —"

Pip bared her teeth and took a step toward her. With a little shriek Marjorie ran into Mr. Romero's workroom. Barian stood there, staring.

"Did you see what Pip did?" Marjorie cried.

"Aw, shut up." Barian poured out the mash. With another gratifying snarl Pip turned away. She had won.

Each morning she and Harold met early to clean the chicken coop until Pip's name was taken from the slot opposite CLEAN COOP and placed at the bottom where she would go without being chicken help until her name rose from slot to slot as they took turns. Only Harold didn't have his name on the list. He kept track of the money, how much was spent for feed for the growing chicks. He wasn't supposed to work with a three-fingered hand.

Pip scarcely believed that her plan had worked so well. She felt a great desire to tell someone about it.

That day she decided to go home by way of the road. The shade in the oak groves was chilly now. All day long it didn't warm up. The road was mostly in the sun. As she set out, she saw Parkman ahead of her. She could tell him. She called out and ran to catch up.

Just as she came within twenty feet of him, Parkman burst into a run and outdistanced her. Then he stopped and walked slowly again.

"Parkman! Wait!" she called and ran again. Again as she came close, he ran ahead. "Wait, Parkman!" she cried out and ran after him. Her breath was getting short, and she had to stop. When she stopped, he stopped but without turning around or letting on he heard her. She turned hot with fury and hated Parkman. She ran after him once more.

This time he let her come even with him. "You wouldn't let me catch up."

Parkman laughed. "I was just trying to stay in the sun."

She knew he was lying, but she didn't know what to say. Parkman always had an answer. She couldn't tell him anything as they crossed under the oaks to the house.

In the living room her mother and Mr. Mehta and three other ladies sat in a ring with their legs crossed. Their eyes were closed, their bare feet on top of their thighs.

"Now we are on the plane of tranquillity," chanted Mr. Mehta. "Inhale —"

Parkman went to the corner of the room and gave three turns to the crank on the windup Victrola.

"Inhale — aaaahhhhhh," breathed Mr. Mehta.

Parkman put on a thick record and spun the turntable.

"Exhale!" chanted Mr. Mehta.

Parkman set the needle on the edge of the record, and the voice of the great tenor Tito Schipa pierced the room in a terrible slowing whine. Her mother's eyes flashed open. "Parkman!" she exclaimed, but he had flown from the room. The record ground downhill, and Schipa's voice wobbled to a stop and died.

Mr. Mehta never opened his eyes. "We cannot stay on the plane of tranquillity with that sort of thing."

"He's gone now," said her mother and closed her eyes again. The other women did the same.

Pip went upstairs. Parkman's door was closed and locked. She tried the knob. "Do you want to trade some pictures?" she called through the crack. There was no answer. She went back to her room and sat down at her desk. Her lined yellow pad lay in front of her. She took up a thick brown pencil and wrote

*Dear Radyar*

She had learned to spell his name from seeing it in the newspaper. She could tell him. She wondered if he would ever come back again.

# 🆑 9 🆑

## The Three Pools

ON SATURDAY MORNING two weeks later her mother had left early with Parkman to go to the dentist in Los Angeles and the house gave off an all-day emptiness. For a while Pip helped Mrs. Hernandez in the kitchen, but she wasn't making anything interesting like candied orange peel or dates stuffed with walnuts as big as her thumb.

She went upstairs and down the hall between the little rooms to the sleeping porch to make her bed. There were two blankets on the bed now, and the covers were heavy. She smoothed the sheet where she could reach it and pulled up the blankets as evenly as possible. She had to crawl across the bed two or three times because the woven blue and white spread kept slipping off on the other side.

When she finished, she went into her room and put her pajamas on the floor of the wardrobe and sat down at her desk. At the top of the lined tablet lying in front of her she wrote

*Dear Daddy*
*How are you? I am fine.*

She couldn't think of anything to tell her father. He seemed not even to be real anymore. She got up and went down the dark oak staircase.

The living room was empty, and the great black fireplace smelled of old fires. The cushions and pillows on the wicker sofas had not been plumped up yet. There were no draperies at the long windows, only the dark shutters which Mrs. Hernandez hadn't opened. Pip unlocked one and pushed it back. Instantly the sun struck the white walls and flooded the room with light. It was like turning on the projector in a dark movie house. Pip closed the shutter and did it again.

She knelt behind the sofa and examined the two boxes of the radio. Taking one knob carefully in her fingers, she moved it. A little light came on in the box and illuminated the dial. She turned the other knob and bent her ear to the other box. Off in the distance she heard a sizzle and snap and crackle. She turned the knob until it wouldn't go any farther and turned it back all the way. The sizzling and crackling were all she could bring in. There weren't any stations on in the morning.

Still the sound was like a fire in a dry Christmas tree, full of snap and sparks. She kept her ear to the speaker as if she might discover secret signals in the sound. And she did. Slowly, growing louder, came a rap-rap-rap. She stiffened to alert, listening, *Rap-Rap-Rap*. Someone was at the front door.

When she opened it, there was Radyar in his tweed jacket and riding breeches and leather puttees, and his helmet.

The goggles he had pushed up above his forehead. He smiled and spread his arms. "Ah, Pip!" he exclaimed.

"Hello, Radyar," Pip regarded him thoughtfully. "Mother isn't here."

Radyar looked unhappy. "Then I can't talk to her. Did you know your mother is very good to talk to?"

Pip said nothing. Sometimes she was, and sometimes she wasn't.

"And I can't invite her on a picnic this beautiful day. May I ask you instead?"

Suddenly she remembered her horoscope. Radyar would tell her future from the stars, and he would know when she was going to die. Her heart thumped, making it difficult to breathe. He might have forgotten, but Radyar did not seem like someone who forgot.

"I'm going to the movies," she said.

"Ask Mr. Radyar in, Pip," Mrs. Hernandez murmured behind her. "It's rude to keep him standing on the step."

Coming inside, Radyar said, "Perhaps you would prefer a picnic to a movie."

"It's Douglas Fairbanks in *The Black Pirate*."

"You don't want to miss that; but we can get back in time if we don't go too far."

"Shall I pack a lunch?" asked Mrs. Hernandez. "Hard-boiled eggs, cold ham and chicken —"

"Ah, chicken," Radyar said.

"We always have chicken," said Pip. "It's what Parkman eats."

"Mrs. dePuyster brought several kinds of fruit yesterday —

pears and grapes and green figs. I'll put in a selection."
Mrs. Hernandez disappeared into the kitchen, while Radyar exclaimed, "Magnificent! A spread to match this day."

He settled back into the sofa. "You seem unusually solemn." When she didn't answer, he went on, "Do you remember pointing out the little road to me? The one that went up into the mountains to the hot springs? I have never been up that way, and I have an urge to do it. Can we find a good picnic place up there?"

"We take a lunch sometimes when we go swimming," Pip said, and Radyar exclaimed, "There we are! It is settled then."

The lunch basket with the Thermos sticking out at an angle fit into the toe of the sidecar on Radyar's motorcycle. Pip had to be careful where she tucked her feet. She didn't want to put a gym shoe into the figs. Mrs. Hernandez watched from the kitchen door while Pip pulled on the extra helmet and set the little round goggles over her eyes.

"Ready?" cried Radyar.

Pip lifted her face and smiled.

"Oh, yes, I remember now. Contact, let 'er go!" he cried. He wheeled the motorcycle around in the drive, roared the motor twice, and made the salute. "We are off and flying!" The motorcycle gathered speed as it went down the hill.

The early morning chill lingered in the shade of the big oaks but in the open places on the road the black tar had begun to smell in the heat. The sun soon made her shoulders hot, and her head in the leather helmet felt sticky, but she didn't care. She wouldn't take it off for anything.

Besides, she needed it for protection. A pebble spinning off the front wheel struck her cheek.

They took the road that wound past her school and joined the main highway beyond the deserted playfield. Now they were out in the full sun. On each side of the road shiny green orange trees were lit with bright round oranges. Between the rows stood metal stoves with tall chimneys, the smudge pots to keep the oranges from freezing on cold winter nights. They were rusty and streaked with smoke.

Over the side Pip observed the brown grass hills and the orange groves and hills again. The speed cooled them as the sun beat down. Pip almost burned her hand on the edge of the sidecar. It had grown that hot.

Then the road narrowed to one lane and began to climb. The hillsides pressed toward them and grew higher. Rocks displaced the grass, and the only trees were little ones. They were in a lower canyon. The road rose sharply. The rocks made it hotter, and the canyon walls cut off the breeze. Radyar pulled into a little side road where a sign read SWIMMING POOL ½ MILE AHEAD.

"We'll have a swim there before lunch."

"I didn't bring my suit," Pip said.

"We will rent suits."

The motorcycle bounced and bounded over the rough road. Radyar wheeled first to one side then the other trying to avoid the worst of the rocks and ruts. Around a narrow bend, the canyon widened into a flat open space where a grove of great sycamores kept all grass from growing.

Through the grove and against the rocky slope lay a huge swimming pool, empty and still under the noonday sun.

"I don't think they're open," Pip said.

"It is late in the year, I suppose." Sitting on the saddle, he watched a moment.

"That pool is awfully cold, anyway," Pip said. "The last time I came swimming here I turned blue on the bottoms of my feet."

"That cold?" exclaimed Radyar. "Then we don't want to swim here, anyway."

"There's the hot springs. It's farther up."

"We go there! *Allons!*"

They went back to the main road and followed it as it wound upward. The surface became rough and rocky, the pavement left behind. Around a bend they were swallowed up in a tunnel. It was dark and cold with the motor's sound echoing through the empty space. In a moment the end appeared, an archway of brilliant light, and they shot out into the sun.

Beyond the tunnel lay another wide flat valley of sycamore trees. Big signs read HOT MINERAL SPRINGS with red zigzags of heat lightning shooting from the word HOT. One sign had fallen down. Pip hoped the pool was still open. She was uncomfortably hot in the sidecar. Dust had sifted over her from her helmet to her gym shoes. And a swim put off again the moment when Radyar would tell her future. He might forget all about it.

A man opened the side of one little stucco house, propping

up the board shutter on a long stick. He pushed two cheap blue swimsuits across the counter for them and pointed to the dressing rooms, GENTLEMEN on one side and LADIES on the other. When Pip came out, she walked across the rough concrete deck and plopped like a stone into the pool. The water lapped over her head and into her hair. For a second she sat on the bottom and felt the water all around her and over her until her chest began to tighten and her stomach hurt. Then she rose to the top like a cork. Radyar was standing up to his waist in water with his hands on his hips.

"This is like swimming in soup," he said. "It's even a little thick."

It was true. The water felt thick. It was warm and gray and murky.

"You never shiver here at all," Pip said. "You won't turn blue."

Radyar laughed.

"I can dive through your legs," said Pip.

"I'll never see you in this murk," he said.

With a jump and a kick Pip dived below the surface, groping for Radyar's legs in the gray water. She slid between them, letting her body slither against his thighs so that he would know she had gone through. Exhilarated, she broke the surface behind him, gasped for air, and dived again. This time she twisted like a barrel roll between his legs, slipping and sliding against him, thrilled with the strength and tension of his muscles. At the moment she came up, he pulled her out and looked at her.

"Could you tell, Radyar?" she cried. "Could you see me?"

"You swim like a little fish." His face was serious. "It's too warm for me, Pip. I'll wait for you."

But it spoiled the fun to have him sitting on the side. She wanted to show him how she could swim underwater, but he couldn't see below the surface. She got up on the diving board to show him how she had learned to dive, crouching on the end of the board with her arms pressed against her ears and her head down and her eyes tight shut. "Radyar! Look!" she called out, and he watched, smiling, but he seemed to be far away. After a short time she gave up and sat down beside him.

"I'm getting hungry," he said. "How about you?" She was, a little. They changed their clothes and got on the motorcycle. "We will find a good place," Radyar said and headed up the road.

Around one bend the canyon became a narrow gorge, the road worsened. Radyar could only go very slowly to avoid the sharpest rocks. When he wheeled to the outside edge of the road, he suddenly exclaimed, "Do you hear something?"

Radyar shut off the motor, and Pip listened. There was a sound like the shower bath running at home.

"There's a waterfall down there! Shall we try to find it?" Radyar took the picnic basket over his arm, and they scrambled down the hillside. "There! Pip, over there where it's green. I'm sure it's in there." The stony soil gave way underfoot, and they slipped. Pip slid five feet on her bottom before they reached the stream bed.

"I'll go first," Radyar said. He pushed his way through

the underbrush, holding back the long branches for her. The stream bed was dry in places and in others it was soft and muddy, squirting up around her gym shoes. They pressed upstream until ahead Radyar exclaimed, "Ah, so beautiful!" She peeked around him and saw an open pool among the white rocks. It was so blue and clear that it looked as if she could touch the stones on the bottom. On the far side a thin waterfall fell from the high white rocks and splashed in the pool below. "It is perfect," Radyar murmured. He set the basket on a smooth white rock and looked into the pool. "This is where we swim."

"I didn't bring my suit," Pip said.

"Nor I," said Radyar. "We can swim in our underwear." He knelt beside the pool and swept his hand through the water. "It is perfect. This sun pocket has kept it just right."

And it was just right. Pip crouched on a smooth white rock on the edge and, leaning over, tumbled into the pool. When she came up, Radyar was out in the middle with just his head sticking out and his wet hair smoothed against his head, laughing with joy.

"It is perfect," he cried. "It proves that only nature can make perfection, which is what I believed all along." Pip dog-paddled all around him.

"I can swim underwater," she said. She kicked two or three times before she managed to dive below the surface. With her eyes wide open she watched the white rocks on the bottom, but they weren't as close as they looked. By the time she touched the largest, smoothest, whitest one, the water had turned quite cold and her chest was tight. She set her feet on the rock and pushed off fast straight up. Radyar had watched all the time floating on his stomach on the surface. "You swim like a little otter," he said. He turned on his back to look up at the sky.

She scrambled along the rocks and found a place to dive. When she looked down and saw the bottom so close, her heart beat hard for a moment, but she knew it was not close. "Radyar! Watch!" she called and fell, pointed arms first, from the rock. Suddenly the water felt funny against her. Something had changed. Looking around she saw that her pants had come off, and now they were slowly sinking toward the deep white rocks. She reached for them but missed.

Her chest was tight. She had to get more air. She bobbed to the surface, gasped and fought to go down again. Her pants now rested on the bottom in a small sandy pocket between two rocks. Kicking hard, she went under but didn't have enough air left. She surfaced again, kicked desperately and went down. The rocks grew bigger and closer. Her hand slid over them and into the pocket, making a fist around her pants. In a second she burst the surface triumphantly and looked to see if Radyar had watched. Radyar sat under the waterfall with his eyes shut and the water sluicing over his head. When she got into her pants, she paddled across the pool and sat beside him.

Later they spread Radyar's jacket on the flattest rock and laid out the thick sandwiches and the hard-boiled eggs and the fruit. The Thermos stood upright wedged between stones. Halfway through his first sandwich Radyar said, "I have been thinking about your horoscope, Pip." He continued to chew while she stopped eating.

"I don't want to disappoint you, but I would like to break my promise."

Pip's heart and stomach squeezed in sudden pain. He must know when she was going to die but didn't want to tell her.

"I am not going to cast any more horoscopes for anyone until I know more — until my new idea is much clearer to me." He bit off more sandwich. "All I wanted at first was to work with Madame Solar, to write her newspaper column for her. Leos, do this! Scorpios, avoid that! I saw a great future for myself. I would be rich and famous. I would be called in by the Hollywood stars. But now — now I am not sure." He finished his sandwich and sat looking across the pool with his arms resting on his knees and his long fingers dangling. "Still, it is something to be famous. The whole world would know the name of Radyar."

Pip watched him carefully. His face did not make her feel that he hid something from her, like the time of her death or his real name. His eyes were serious and distant now, but in a second they would be bright and laughing again.

"Is your name really Radyar?" she asked.

His eyes quickened as he looked at her. "Do you know what my real name is?" he said. "Hiram Joseph Smith. Yes, that is it. Hiram Joseph Smith."

A little electric shock of disappointment went through Pip.

"I hated my name, Pip. I felt doomed to act like someone named Hiram Joseph Smith. Have you ever heard of anyone interesting with such a name? Of course you haven't. So I decided to change it, and I tried a dozen, like trying on new clothes. Houdini, Khayyam, Sergei Dimitri Tolstoyevsky, but they were too fantastic. Then Radyar came to me. Just one word — Radyar. It sounded so confident, so Rumanian. And it went with being an astrologer. So I left my hometown, a place much worse than Kansas City, and came here to the Golden State to a new life, to Madame Solar and now to a new vision."

"What's a vision?"

"It is a picture in your head which is so vivid it is like seeing it in front of your eyes, but it is not like a picture of blue sky and trees. It is a way of understanding the world. My vision tells me there is something more to astrology than Leos do this today, Scorpios don't do that." Radyar frowned and spoke vehemently. "That is based on fear, Pip, people's fear of the future, of what may happen."

"Like when they're going to die?" Pip asked.

"Yes! And fear is a terrible thing. Fear crushes life, Pip, and we must not crush life."

Pip watched him silently for several minutes. "Parkman says stars are just stars," she said, "and don't do anything to people."

Radyar nodded. "Many people believe that, and if you believe that stars are just stars, then they are just stars. I believe they are more than that. How can it be otherwise, Pip? The heavens are so beautiful! Day and night, light and dark, sun and moon and planets and stars. Without sun we die. We have no food. Without night we die. We must sleep. The earth must not burn up. Warmth and cold, the seasons — all these things we owe to the heavens. They guide us, tell us when to plant, when to harvest. All the important things. I see the heavens and earth put together, and I believe in their guidance. The world is all one, Pip. Humans and earth and sky and sunfire and cool water — we are knit together, into one universe," he lifted his arms and spread them outward, "into one great world." His arms fell, and he stretched out on his back on the rock.

The white rocks folded like bread dough around them, the blue sky stretched overhead, the water fell into the little pool, and the sun warmed them all. The world was one and whole. Radyar said it could not be otherwise, and she believed him.

The waterfall splashed in the still warm air, making the only sound. After a few minutes, Pip asked, "Are you still going to hunt for a fortune?"

Like a shot Radyar sat up. "What? What makes you say that?"

Pip was so startled that she jumped a little. Radyar stared at her, his eyes hard as blue glass. "Ah. So that is what they are saying, the laughing Andrea and the beautiful Dorrit."

"Parkman said it." Radyar groaned. "He heard them talking."

"I suppose they said I am looking for a rich woman to marry." He fixed his hard blue eyes on Pip, making her

squirm without speaking. "Yes, that is what they think."
He picked up a stone and heaved it angrily into the pool,
smashing its surface. "It's not a bad idea. Maybe I will."

"My mother's just as rich as Aunt Andrea," Pip said.
Radyar stopped with the Thermos halfway to his mouth.
His blue eyes softened. "And she is more beautiful and
more intelligent, and she has you." Pip watched him drink
from the bottle.

When he finished, they packed the basket again and
scrambled upward through the underbrush and over the
rocks to the motorcycle and set out for home.

"I'm afraid we missed *The Black Pirate*," Radyar said. He
pushed his sleeve back from his huge wristwatch and studied
the face. "Three-fifteen. It must be half over."

"I don't mind," Pip said. Now that she remembered, she
felt some disappointment, but she hadn't even thought of
it until then.

Her mother and Parkman were still away when they got
home, and Radyar would not wait. Pip watched him turn
the motorcycle around in the drive, wondering if he hated
her mother now and if he would ever come back. She held
out her hand. "Good-bye, Radyar."

He took her hand in both of his for a minute, looking at
her, and his eyes were as blue and clear as the pool below
the waterfall. "Perhaps I am a black pirate," he said. With
his white teeth flashing, his eyes suddenly electric, he looked
like Douglas Fairbanks for a moment. Then he turned up
the gas and shot down the drive with a roar.

The house was still quiet but not vacant in the way it had been in the morning. Sitting at her desk, Pip finished her letter to her father, telling him about the picnic and swimming in the pool with the waterfall and Radyar and the motorcycle. She was just signing her name when she heard her mother's roadster in the driveway.

# ◈ 10 ◈

## Parkman

WHEN PIP CAME DOWNSTAIRS the next morning, Parkman was already curled up in a living room chair, his new book about eight inches from his face. Pip wondered if he really would ruin his eyes holding it so close, and she wondered what ruined eyes looked like, imagining them in the palm of her hand like crushed colored marbles turned to jelly. She went to the table under the window and ate her breakfast. The blue peasant woman appeared on the bottom of her cereal bowl just as Parkman slapped the covers of the book together.

"Boy, was that ever good!"

"What was it about?"

"This boy, Bradford, goes all over the Alps mountains, they're like the Rockies only they're in Switzerland, and he goes exploring and climbing the glaciers and everything. He's only two years older than I am."

"Can he write a book?" Pip asked.

"Maybe somebody helped him. He goes with his father." Parkman looked gloomy. "I wish I had a father like that."

Pip wondered what such a father would be like. Fathers were men who went to the office every day and didn't know anything about you. It hadn't occurred to her that other fathers might be different. Even Marjorie Steadman's father who ran the drugstore was always in the drugstore. She had never seen him at home or with Marjorie.

"I wish I could go to the Alps," Parkman said.

Pip knew in a split second that this was one of the days when she could be close to Parkman.

"We could fly there," she said.

Staring straight ahead, Parkman began to make noises like an airplane motor warming up. He closed his hand on the joystick hardly giving Pip time to climb into the open cockpit behind him before he pulled back the stick and the nose of the plane rose into the air.

Parkman piloted the plane like a maddened bird, shooting straight up, whining straight down, doing loop-the-loops which were his favorite, and finally flying upside down ten feet above the earth before he righted the plane again. Shrieking, Pip felt her heart pound the way it did in an Al Wilson movie. When he wanted to, Parkman could make you believe anything. It was just that he didn't want to very often. With arms spread wide they zoomed out the door and around the house three times before they came to rest on the edge of a glacier just off the terrace. Parkman climbed from the cockpit and sunk his ax into the glacial ice of the white sycamore tree.

"If we can just make an ice cave," he panted, pulling himself upward over the smooth white bark, "we can live through this blizzard."

It wasn't an easy climb. The sycamore had no little cracks

in the bark like an oak where Pip could stick her toe. It
was smooth as ice and slippery. Once they had gained the
crotch where the three limbs branched off, Parkman said,
"This way," as if the limb were a trail over the glacier. He
walked out on it and let himself down into the hollow.

They settled in, with only their heads and shoulders
showing. Pip leaned back and looked up through the leaves.
The sky was a bright and empty blue, the way the sky above
a glacier would be, she thought. They sat for a long time
without speaking.

"What did you do with Radyar yesterday?"

The ice cave disappeared. She told him about the picnic
high up on the hot springs road where they had found the
waterfall and gone swimming in their underwear. Parkman
grinned foolishly when he heard that. "You went swimming
in your underpants?"

"They only came off once," Pip said. Parkman nearly
fell out of the tree laughing and began to chant, "Pip lost
her underpants, Pip lost her underpants."

"I got them back. I dived way down to the rocks, Parkman. It was so deep my head hurt."

Parkman stopped chanting, obviously impressed. "Being
buried in an avalanche must be like that."

They sat in silence again.

"Parkman," she said, "look up there." She pointed to the
trunk above their heads. In the bark were rows of holes half
an inch deep as regular in rows and size as if someone had
made them with a drill. Into each hole an acorn had been
pushed.

"It must be a squirrel's cupboard," she said.

Parkman studied them for a few minutes. "A squirrel can't do that. I'll bet the woodpecker did it."

"Woodpeckers are awfully dumb," Pip said.

Then Parkman began to laugh. "That woodpecker is so dumb he's trying to make a new tree. He's trying to make a sycacorn."

"Or an acamore," said Pip.

"A sycamoak!"

"An oakamore!"

They laughed and laughed and thought of all the names they could. Times like these she was happy and loved Parkman and forgot the other times when she hated him and could scream with fury.

When their mother came out on the porch for lunch, Pip began eagerly to tell her, but Parkman grew sullen and angry and said scornfully, "You can't make a new tree." Pip's high spirits fell in confusion. Parkman had gone back to his other way, and she could not change it. She stopped talking and laughing and ate her soup.

"But I do think it is worth trying to make a new tree," said her mother gently, folding her sweater about her as it was chilly even in the sun.

That night after dinner Parkman got down behind the sofa and worked the radio dials until they could hear scratchy voices singing "East side, west side, all around the town." When the song was over, they listened to the voice of Al Smith who wanted to be President of the United States.

"I do hope he wins," said her mother. "He is so full of vitality." Pip wondered what anyone with such a voice could be like. Someone was singing "Yes sir, you're my baby, no sir, I don't mean maybe, yes sir, you're my baby naow" when her mother sent her up to bed.

The floor of the sleeping porch was cold under her bare feet, and she jumped up on Parkman's bed to leap across to hers. By sliding between the sheets without opening the covers she kept out most of the cold air. She lay still in one place until it warmed up. Then she relaxed and moved a little to warm up a wider space.

# ☙ 11 ❧

## The Daredevil of the Sky

WHEN MR. ZICK'S DOOR OPENED, Pip noticed a new smell besides the steam and eucalyptus oil that rolled out of the office.

"Hello, Mr. Zick. It's me, Pip."

"Well, if it isn't," said Mr. Zick, wiping his bald head. "You missed it last week, a great picture, one of the greatest, Pip."

"I went on a picnic."

At that moment the steam stirred, and Mrs. Huckaby beat her way through the door. "Hello, Pip."

"Hello, Mrs. Huckaby." Pip was surprised to see her.

"Mr. Zick liked the nut loaf so much I'm trying out a new soup on him. Like a taste?"

Pip said she would. She wondered where Mrs. Huckaby found a place to cook in Mr. Zick's office. It wasn't easy to breathe or see even if she fanned fast in front of her face. Then things were piled everywhere, on the desk and the chairs and the floor, and the office wasn't big to begin with.

Once she stepped inside, she found that Mrs. Huckaby had made room. For one thing she had Mr. Zick's eucalyptus oil tea kettle singing on a hot plate on the desk.

Stuck on the spout was a long cardboard cylinder which she told him to sit by so the steam didn't have to fill the whole room. Another hot plate sat on the end of an upturned orange crate, and on it the thick soup bubbled, big blisters forming and breaking. Mrs. Huckaby dipped into it and filled a thick white cup halfway. Mr. Zick sat down at the desk and took two or three breaths through the tube.

"Did you know Mr. Zick all the time?" Pip asked, watching the hot soup warily.

"She followed up on the malted nuts, Pip. That's the way to make a sale." He took the cardboard tube and swatted Mrs. Huckaby's behind. "First the free sample, then the pitch."

"Try your soup, Ezekiel, it'll loosen your chest."

"That will be a soup," Mr. Zick said, taking a sip. Mrs. Huckaby watched his face. "It's all right," he said, "I like it, not like my mother's, but all right."

"It's all natural ingredients, everything fresh, just a teaspoon of Savita for flavor. What do you think, Pip?"

"It's delicious, Mrs. Huckaby." She scraped out the lumps with her finger and licked it.

"I'll give Mrs. Hernandez the receipt."

Finishing his soup, Mr. Zick took a long breath through the tube and then wiped away the steam fogging his glasses. "I have news for you, Pip. He's coming. I got it special for you. It's his latest, Pip. Guess who."

Pip could hardly breathe for a moment. "Is it Al Wilson?" she whispered.

"Al Wilson, the Daredevil of the Sky," said Mr. Zick. "In this one he jumps off a burning plane, Pip." Mr. Zick's voice had magic in it. "There are more loop-the-loops and tailspins and spiral nose dives than in all the other Al Wilson pictures put together. That's what they say, Pip. I haven't seen it."

"I'm coming." Pip set her cup on the orange crate. "When will it be here?"

"Next Saturday, Pip, a special matinee. Tell your friends. It's the greatest thrill treat of the year. It's got everything, even racing cars."

"Parkman likes those," Pip said. "He'll come, too. I know he will."

The three of them carried the stacks of old show pictures to Pip's wagon. Mrs. Huckaby put an extra pile in her basket which was now almost empty because Mr. Zick had bought several boxes of vegetized crackers, a jar of malted nuts, and two packages of unsulfured dried apricots which, Mrs. Huckaby said, were healthier than sulfured ones. She helped Pip pull the wagon on the uphill stretch. They parted where the driveways met the road, Mrs. Huckaby going up hers and Pip pulling the wagon up to the oak beside the garage. She wondered how she could wait till next Saturday.

She had never been up in an airplane. All that she knew about airplanes she had learned from movies and show pictures and from Parkman who had read everything about Colonel Charles A. Lindbergh. Once last summer her father had driven her out to a landing field near Kansas City and let her look at two little planes that were parked there. "Now are you satisfied?" he asked, and she couldn't answer. He had laughed and said, "Why does a little girl like you have to know about airplanes?" After that she knew that she could never tell him.

The week dragged slowly. Each day seemed stuck in heavy mud. It was as hard as waiting for Christmas morning. No, it was worse. Pip wanted to run against the wall of time and push it ahead of her. But there was nothing to push. She had to bear the unbearable and let each day evaporate into the next which they did one by one until Saturday came.

"Eat your lunch, Pip," Mrs. Hernandez urged her. "For a movie like this you need the nourishment."

But she couldn't. Her plate sat in front of her, hardly touched.

"If you're coming, hurry up and eat," Parkman said.

"I'm coming."

Suddenly she left the table and ran upstairs to her room. It occurred to her that she should not wear coveralls to this movie. Quickly she unbuttoned the red buttons and left the coveralls like two whirlpools on the floor. She opened the wardrobe which didn't have much in it and took down her blue embroidered dress. It was the best dress she had, the only one that fit anymore, and it was the only dress to wear to see the daredevil of the sky. But it didn't look much like what an aviator or an aviatrix might wear. Just as quickly she took off the dress and jumped into the puddled legs of the coveralls and pulled them up. Parkman was yelling, "I won't wait unless you get down here in two seconds."

"I'm coming," she yelled, buttoning the red buttons and snatching up her red sweater. She flew down the stairs.

Parkman was already going down the drive. "Wait for me, Parkman!" She hated to have to trot after him, never catching up. At that moment Parkman stopped and held out his arm to her. The tarantula was crossing the drive, tiptoeing on its arched hairy legs. Under the bright sun it looked more brown than black. They waited until it stepped into the grass, and then Parkman said, "Come on," and broke into a run. In a few seconds he was way ahead of her She had a cramp in her side, too, which she pressed with her hand as hard as she could.

"We'll be late. We'll miss the beginning." He ran again.

Pip scowled miserably. Her side hurt no matter how much she pressed it. She tried to walk fast but couldn't. It was impossible to run more than a few steps. What with changing her clothes twice and then the tarantula, she would miss the first part and she felt like crying. Already Parkman was out of sight around the hill.

"Hello, Pip," Bill Tanner stopped his milk truck beside her. "Where you going?"

"Hello, Mr. Tanner. To the Paramount."

"Hop in. I'm going through town to the dairy. I can give you a lift."

Pip promised herself that she would always give him the

salute for friends from now on. She climbed through the open door into the milk truck.

"Hang onto the bar there," Bill Tanner said. "This buggy can be bumpy."

"I know where all the bumps are," Pip said.

"I'll bet you do. You've hit them all in that wagon, I'll bet."

The back of the truck was stacked with worn wooden milk boxes. Some of them jingled with empty bottles. Melting ice darkened the floor. In front of her the big window gave a wide view of the street. Looking through it made the world into a new place like a picture in a big frame.

Parkman was walking along the sidewalk when they passed him. She held on with one hand and gave him the salute with her right. He looked up once and then quickly again, his mouth open. Suddenly the pain left her side, and she felt very much better.

"You can let me off at the corner," she said.

"I'm in no hurry," Bill Tanner said. "I'm used to giving curb service."

When he turned the corner, Pip could see the marquee over the Paramount entrance. AL WILSON, it read, THE DAREDEVIL OF THE SKY, ONE APPEARANCE, SAT. MAT. ONLY. Under it she saw Barian and Marjorie and Harold in the milling crowd. Bill Tanner pulled up in front. Everyone watched as she stepped down from the milk truck.

"Thank you, Mr. Tanner."

"My pleasure," he said.

For a minute Marjorie stopped jumping up and down in front of Barian to stare.

"Does he give you a ride all the time, Pip?" Barian asked, following her to the ticket office. Harold attached himself to her. Pip wished he wouldn't, but she could not bring herself to tell him to go away. She had promised to be his real friend. Now she must do it. Without looking at anyone she marched up to the ticket window.

"Is it fifteen cents or a quarter, Mr. Zick?" asked.

"Sad to say, a quarter, but it's worth every penny."

She believed it. Barian pushed his money through the half-moon window, and then Marjorie. Harold already had his orange ticket closed in his three-fingered hand.

Pip led the way through the crowd to the doors which opened as she reached them. Mrs. Huckaby swung them back and kicked the wedge doorstops underneath. Then she took the place by the ticket collection stand. Pip was the first in line.

Mrs. Huckaby took her orange ticket, tore it in half and dropped one half into the collection stand while she gave the other back to Pip. "Thrills galore, Pip. You'll need your good health," she said, reaching out for Harold's ticket.

They were the first in the theater. Pip marched down the aisle and chose the row halfway back which she liked best. She took the aisle seat, and the others climbed over her legs getting by. Harold sat down next to her, and Barian plopped into his lap. Marjorie was stuck standing on Pip's foot. They made her very angry. She gave Marjorie a shove just as Harold tried to shove Barian, and the two of them tumbled between the seats, screaming with laughter.

By then the whole theater was shrieking, and Pip covered her ears against the sound. Barian passed his white paper bag of mint leaves in front of her. Taking one fast, she covered her ears again. Marjorie tried to climb out to see somebody, but Pip yelled at her to sit down so she did. Barian made spitballs from the bag and threw them. Only Harold sat still, leaning against her shoulder, his thin legs sticking straight out in front of him. She tried to shrug him off, but he only settled against her again.

The shrieking and scraping rose to an almost unbearable pitch. Pip's ears ached with the pressure of her hands over them. Then suddenly the theater went black, and the screams increased. She thought her head would fly off on the waves of sound. The giant screen flickered with scratches of light, and then the title flashed before her eyes: AL WILSON IN and then on the next flash, THREE MILES UP. The voices shrieked higher, and Pip put one hand on her head to hold it on and pressed the other against her chest to keep it from exploding. She was screaming, too.

It was true. There were thrills galore, more tailspins and loop-the-loops and nose dives and spirals than in all the Al Wilson movies put together, almost more than Pip could bear. Sweat sprang from her scalp when Al Wilson walked out on the lower wing of the biplane, hanging on to the struts, almost falling over the edge. When the plane swooped low over the racing car, Harold cried out, "He'll get hurt, won't he, Pip?" and she couldn't make her mouth answer. One plane spiraled downward bursting with flames, the whine of the engine louder than the shrieking crowd. It exploded behind a barn. She saw Al Wilson grinning from ear to ear as his plane zipped along upside down. He lifted his gloved hand and touched the edge of his goggles. Pip, on the edge of her seat with Harold clutching her arm, lifted her free hand in reply.

When the flickering screen said THE END and the music stopped and the lights sprang on in the theater, everyone around her jumped up and ran shrieking up the aisle. Pip could hardly move. Harold still gripped the seat with both hands. Barian and Marjorie tried to push past their legs. Pip placed a good kick on Barian's shin. "Wait a minute," she yelled at him. He sat down on Harold again, too surprised to howl.

Pip sat still until the aisle was free, and then she got up and led the three of them out. Mr. Zick and Mrs. Huckaby stood at the doors, giving people little helping pushes through.

"How you like it, Pip?" asked Mr. Zick.

Her voice was hoarse and her throat ached. Her head hurt and her ears were tender. By trying hard, she managed to say, "It's the best movie you've ever had, Mr. Zick."

"I knew you'd like it. A pip of a picture I said as soon as I heard about it."

The sunlight pierced her eyes and made her head hurt more. When Mrs. Steadman offered her a ride home in the black Ford motorcar she climbed in back without saying a word. Barian and Marjorie began to tell all about the movie, while Pip sank against the prickly upholstery. Harold snuggled beside her.

"Do you think I can be an aviator?" Harold whispered. He held up his three-fingered hand and looked into Pip's face. Suddenly, alone and quiet in the backseat she felt very close to Harold. She knew that they were real friends. "You can fly with me all you want," she said. Sighing, Harold relaxed against her.

It wasn't until later that she realized she had lost her sweater at the movies.

# ☖ 12 ☖

## Dead Horse Valley

**P**IP STILL could not say much at dinner time. When Mrs. Hernandez remarked about her silence, anger bubbled inside her. The memory and the feelings and the sensations of the afternoon she protected as best she could and ignored Parkman's poke. Her mother asked him, "Didn't you like the movie?" He was silent, and Pip knew he had liked it. How could he help it? But no one, no one, she was certain, felt the way she did. Halfway through dessert she sank back in her chair, asleep.

It was the middle of the week before she could bring herself to look at the pictures of Al Wilson tacked to the wardrobe door. The still, shiny photographs had lost something. The pictures had to move. The wind had to whip Al Wilson's scarf as he stood on the wing of the plane. His smile had to come and go while he hung upside down in the cockpit. The flames had to crackle, the noise whine louder and higher as the fragile plane plummeted toward the earth.

By Saturday she managed to leaf through the stack of photographs on her desk, setting aside only three that she liked. Even those didn't bring back Saturday's matinee.

She looked out the window and watched the turtle making its slow way from the tub of green water to the edge of the garage roof. It gave her the idea that it was a good day to go out.

She left her room, went down the stairs and pulled her wagon from the garage, checked its moving parts, and coasted down the drive. At the road she did not turn right as she would if she wanted a long coast or to go to the village. She steered to the left. After a few feet the wagon came to a stop.

Pip pulled it behind her under the row of acacia trees and then took first a left then a right turn on the wandering road. It was now November, the ground dry, the grass under the trees brown. The vistas through the grove were long and open, sometimes showing a house at the far end. Pulling the wagon she walked on.

It was not easy going. The road climbed a little all the time, and after a while it came out of the trees at the edge of the open brown foothills. Pip had never been there before. When she came to a dusty road leading into the hills, she took it.

The going grew rougher. The wheels sank in the loose dirt, making the wagon hard to pull. There were no trees for shade. Pip worked two wheels onto the grassy center between the ruts which made the pulling a little easier.

As the road wound between the low hills, the ruts themselves had grass growing in them. The road had not been used in a long, long time.

Around her there wasn't much to see, some chunks of

rotting wood, occasional clumps of tall grass, and sometimes a bone. Pip made up her mind to round one more bend and rest and turn back.

She stopped beside a huge leg bone and studied it. It was white and the surface was pitted. She picked it up — it was not particularly heavy — and put it in the wagon.

Now there were more bones on both sides of the wheel tracks. The shallow valley widened between the hills, and it was white with bones. They were all over! Pip pulled her wagon farther along the ruts. Beside her, ahead of her, everywhere were bones, gleaming white in the sun.

"Horses!"

She left her wagon and went over to a huge skull. It lay on the ground as if the horse had rested its head there and never moved again. The skull was long and narrow and horselike. A cow would have horns. She set the skull upright and looked into the eye sockets. They were hollow and smooth to her fingers.

Beyond the skull a great rib cage lay in the grass. Pip crawled inside. Lying on her back, she looked up through the rib bones at the blue sky. It was like being in a house that isn't all built yet and looking up at the sky through the rafters of the roof. No, it was more like being in a glass-bottomed boat and looking through the ribs into the deepest, emptiest sea. She lay still and wondered where the fish would be.

She crawled out and pulled and worked on the rib cage until the backbone was straight up and the ribs held it. She crawled underneath and rolled over again. Now it was like

a house with the roof beam in place. She lay very still thinking, and she did not realize for several minutes that she was
no longer looking up into the empty sky but into Yamaji's
dark face. Her heart suddenly speeded up.

Yamaji smiled. His teeth were very white in his brown
face. "So — you like bones, too," he said.

Pip scrambled to her feet.

"Hello, Mr. Yamaji."

"Hello, Pip. I didn't know you walked here."

"I've never been here before today. I just found it."

"Is that so? I walk here almost everyday. Bones help me
think."

"Like the sycamore tree?" Pip said, and Yamaji nodded.
He clasped his brown hands behind his back, and they
walked side by side along the wagon ruts.

"It's a horse graveyard," Pip said.

"It has not been used for a long time," said Yamaji. "The
bones are not new. They are very old bones."

"Horses go to a place they know to die," Pip said. "Parkman told me that."

"Do they? I didn't know. I wondered how they came to
be here. I thought perhaps horse owners had brought their
sick animals here and had shot them — a long time ago, of
course. There is no sign of violent death. The bones are
not even disarranged very much by wild animals or vul-
tures."

They stopped by a full skeleton lying on its side. Even
the tail vertebrae were in place. Only one leg bone was
missing.

"Feel them," said Pip. "They feel funny."

Yamaji picked up a stray rib and drew it across his hand. His palm was a lighter brown than the back. The rib bone was flat and rounded on the edges, and it curved like a barrel stave. He handed it to Pip who stroked it on her palm. It was smooth and chalky and it had a honeycomb of pits in its surface.

"Isn't that strange?" asked Yamaji. "How can a bone have little holes in it and still feel smooth and have a chalky surface and be silky too?"

Pip looked up at him and smiled. "It's funny."

"It is part of the strangeness of bones," he said.

Rocks poked through the soil and grass here and there among the skeletons. The ground rose gently toward the hills.

"Bones have a long life," said Yamaji.

"But bones aren't alive, are they?"

"In our bodies they live. They grow. If they didn't, you would not be bigger year by year until someday you will be as tall as I am, taller perhaps."

"And babies would never get any bigger," said Pip.

"Then when the body dies, our flesh and blood and hair vanish very quickly, but the bones live on. Not growing as they did, of course, but existing, remaining. It fills me with wonder."

"Me, too," said Pip who had not thought of it before, but she found that she wondered, too.

At the head of the valley the hills closed in again. The bones were fewer and more scattered about. A twisted live oak grew there, and under it a dead limb lay where it had fallen.

"I usually sit here before I go back," Yamaji said. "Will you stay with me?"

Pip sat down on the dead branch and looked at her companion. He wore his loose white shirt and white pants again. She had never seen him in anything else. He took a deep breath, and she did, too, sighing as she let it out.

"Bones don't frighten you, I see."

"Oh, no." She hadn't thought of being frightened at all. "They aren't scary. Things that move are scary, things that move fast."

Yamaji laughed. "Yes, that is true. We are most frightened when we are taken by surprise."

They looked over the open meadow. There was no telling how many horses had left their skeletons behind there.

"Are you still thinking about being a great man?" Pip asked.

Yamaji smiled gently and lifted one hand in a little wave toward the bones. "I am not much interested in being a great man. I want to find the strongest, most lasting things, the thoughts like bones."

"Is it kind of a vision?"

Yamaji looked at her in some surprise. "Yes, a vision. And you — did you find a way through your difficulties in being chicken help?"

Then she told him about her plan and about Harold who had only three fingers on one hand and no friends and how she had promised to be his friend if he cleaned the coop when her turn came, and how he did it and they were friends even though she hadn't meant to be really at first. When she finished, Yamaji did not speak for several minutes. "The little boy, Harold — he is quite as useful to you as if he were a chicken."

Pip stared at Yamaji, her hand coming to her mouth. "But I don't want Harold to be a chicken. I wouldn't be a chicken for anything."

"Perhaps there is another way," Yamaji said, but Pip didn't know what it was. She saw herself raking up the dust and chicken droppings and not being able to breathe, and she bit her lip. She couldn't do it. Still she did not want to turn anyone else into a chicken. Feeling nervous and puzzled, she stood up. "I have to go home for lunch."

"Let us walk to the road together," Yamaji said.

"Would you mind carrying a skull for me? I want to put it in my wagon."

"Not at all," he said. "Have you picked one out?"

"I'm going to." Pip wandered back and forth across the meadow, examining the skulls. Some were bigger than others. Some were longer, some narrower, some wider between the eye sockets. The bumpy ridge on the forehead was higher in some. She settled for one with the smoothest feeling of silk and chalk, and Yamaji tucked it under his arm.

When they came to her wagon, he placed it carefully in the wagon bed and laid the rib bone beside it. She needed help in turning the wagon around in the loose sand. Yamaji took the tongue in his brown hand and pulled the wagon to the place where the dirt road joined the blacktop.

"I have enjoyed our walk, Pip," he said. "It was very pleasant meeting you again."

"Thank you, Mr. Yamaji." Pip held out her hand, and they shook.

"I hope you'll join me another time. I walk here almost every day late in the morning."

"I will. Thank you for helping me with my wagon."

"You are most welcome. Now, I go this way. You should hurry to be home for lunch. Good-bye."

"Good-bye, Mr. Yamaji."

Pip watched as he walked away from her up the blacktop road. At the top of the rise he turned and waved. She waved back, and he disappeared behind the hill. Then she arranged the skull at the back of the wagon, set the rib bone along the side, knelt on one knee, and, pushing off with the other foot, began to coast down the hill. Somehow she did not feel comfortable. A picture of Harold half-clucking and pawing after her across the chicken yard disturbed her. She had done a terrible wrong to him, but without him she would do a worse thing to herself.

With the skull and rib bone in her arms Pip kicked the back screen door. "Mrs. Hernandez, will you please open the screen?"

"Aye-yie!" Mrs. Hernandez exclaimed as Pip pushed past her. "What do you want with such things, a nice little girl like you? Leave those outside by the garbage can."

"I'm going to put them in my room. You don't have to look."

"One more and you'll have a skull and crossbones."

Pip turned and looked at her. "I didn't think of that." She would have to go back. "Where's Mother?"

"She has gone to lunch at Mr. Livingstone's."

"Did Parkman go with her?"

"Parkman is reading on the veranda. Lunch will be ready in a few minutes. You wash your hands after touching those."

"They aren't dirty."

"You wash, anyway."

Pip carried the bones upstairs and into her room. By moving the chair there was a place to prop the skull up in the corner. She needed a way to hang it on the wall. Then she could cross two rib bones below it. After lunch maybe Parkman would help her. If she kept busy, she would not think about Harold.

# ◙ 13 ◙

## Mr. Livingstone Weeps

HER NAME on the cardboard piece had risen slot by slot until again it was opposite CLEAN COOP and still she had not been able to think of another way to get out of raking the chicken droppings herself. When her morning came, she rounded the school building early to find Harold already there. He had taken the rake from Mr. Romero's workroom and had begun. He hummed as he worked. She pressed against the chicken wire, watching, trying to think.

"Hello, Pip."

She entered the coop. "Give me the rake," she said, and Harold stopped to stare at her.

"Don't you like me anymore? Aren't we friends?"

Pip looked away, shuffling her gym shoes in the dust. "We're friends, that's all right, but I have to rake. It's my turn."

"But I want to do it," Harold said, holding as tight as he could to the handle as she tugged on it. "Nobody thinks I can do things like this, but I can!" Harold's eyes glistened. "You're the only one who ever lets me."

Pip let go of the handle. "You like raking?"

Harold nodded. Pip put her hand to her mouth, wondering, while he tightened his grip. "I can do it, Pip, even if I do only have three fingers!" Pip went outside and sat down on Mr. Romero's bench. Harold was humming again. She didn't know what to think, but she knew they both were happy.

All day she was relieved and content, and when she got home, her thoughts and feelings occupied her so completely that for several minutes she stared at the people gathered in the living room, unable to understand what was happening there.

Her mother knelt on the floor in front of the sofa, and her hands covered Mr. Livingstone's where they rested on his knees. His head was thrown back, his pointed gray beard thrust out. His eyes were tight shut, and tears stood on his cheeks.

"I'm sure it's not true!" her mother exclaimed. "I'm sure, Thomas."

"No, no, Dorrit," Mr. Livingstone gasped. "Yamaji has left me. He has deserted me." Freeing one hand from hers he felt for the white handkerchief which peeped from the breast pocket of his gray coat and pressed it to his eyes and cheeks and moustache.

Pip tiptoed to the staircase, turned around the newel post and mounted the stairs one slow step at a time, watching over the banister all the while.

Her mother stood up, brushing back her thick hair, and held out her hands to Mrs. Livingstone who sat in an armchair. Mr. Livingstone drew deep rasping breaths in the silence.

Pip had never seen a grown-up cry before, and the shock set her stomach trembling. She tightened her hold on the banister as she looked over it. The silence continued for so long that she was afraid they would hear her own breathing, and she tiptoed around the top of the stairs to Parkman's door. He sat on the floor with his collection of movie pictures spread out around him.

"Look out where you're walking," he whispered.

Pip closed his door behind her, listening for the little click of the lock. "What's the matter with Mr. Livingstone?" she whispered. Her lips trembled.

"That big baby," Parkman said. He laid a Rudolph Valentino picture on top of a Rin Tin Tin.

"They don't go together," Pip said.

"They do, too. They both start with R, dummy."

So that was how Parkman made his piles, alphabetically. No wonder he had so many. There wasn't room to walk around. Pip sat down against the door. "It's something awfully bad." Parkman just growled and continued to deal out his photographs. Pip tried again. "Something terrible has happened. He wouldn't cry like that."

"Crazy people cry all the time," said Parkman.

Pip shivered. Was Mr. Livingstone really crazy? Until now he had never acted funny. Carefully she opened the door and slipped out. By squatting behind the banister she could see into the living room below.

Her mother sat next to Mr. Livingstone on the sofa, holding one of his hands in both of hers. Mrs. Livingstone held his cane and his huge white Panama hat on her lap. For the moment the group was silent.

Mr. Livingstone tucked his handkerchief back into his breast pocket. "You understand what this does — this desertion."

"Yes — yes," murmured her mother.

"My vision — my vision is destroyed."

"It is not desertion," whispered Mrs. Livingstone. "It is betrayal!" Her cushiony body trembled.

"Give me my stick, my dear. We have gone over this enough. Dorrit understands what has happened. It is a great shock." He rose from the couch, took his cane and rested for a moment against it. "My dear, thank you for your comfort, your understanding."

Mrs. Livingstone kissed her mother's cheek. "He takes it so much better than I do. I would simply tear Yamaji to pieces with my teeth, if I should see him."

"So vicious, my dear," and Mr. Livingstone laughed a little. "It is what we teach against."

At the door Mrs. Livingstone gave him his great hat, and her mother closed the heavy door behind them. With her hands still on the knob, she leaned her back against the dark oak. She drew a long breath, and looking up her eyes caught Pip seated on the top step. "Oh, my, this is a shock, Pip. Poor Mr. Livingstone."

Pip came downstairs and followed her mother across the living room. Her mother sank into one end of the sofa, and

Pip sat rigidly on the edge of a cushion. The tea tray still stood on the little table. "They didn't drink their tea," Pip said.

"They were too upset. They are very hurt." Her mother poured a cup of tea for herself and held out a plate of coconut puffs for Pip who shook her head.

"Is Mr. Yamaji a bad man?"

"Oh, no, darling, not at all. He is a great man, a great teacher. For ten years Thomas Livingstone has helped him go all over the world teaching and speaking, and now Yamaji has broken away from him."

In her head Pip saw the white-clad Yamaji turn at the top of the hill and wave to her. He looked so small and alone.

"I wish I could talk with him," said her mother. "Perhaps he can be persuaded. Perhaps he doesn't realize how much people all over the world are counting on him, believing in him. If someone could tell him, I know he would listen, but the Livingstones say no one has seen him since he made his decision. Mr. Mehta is with him and won't let anyone in the house. He answers the telephone for Yamaji. It is impossible to get to him."

"I see him sometimes," Pip said. Her mother set down her tea cup, saying, "You and your imagination, Pip."

"I do, too!" Pip said.

"Oh, Pip," and her mother laughed. Pip was shocked that her mother didn't believe her. Her insides which had quieted down gave a startling jerk.

"All right, where do you see Mr. Yamaji sometimes?"

"He walks everyday in Dead Horse Valley."

"How do you know that? You're in school everyday."

"He told me. I see him there on Saturdays."

"And where is Dead Horse Valley?" asked her mother. "I've never heard of it."

"It's where I got the skull and the rib bone."

Her mother sat up, her eyes growing larger. "Of course, I'd forgotten them. Are you sure, Pip? That he walks there everyday?"

"He said so when he helped me with the bones."

"Oh, Pip, can you find the place again? If I could just talk with him so that he understands how hurt Mr. Livingstone is. He might change his mind. Tomorrow, Pip, can you take me there? Do you know the way?"

She was a little insulted that her mother should ask such a question. "I need one more bone," she said.

The middle of the next morning Pip sat on the back doorstep waiting for her mother and watched the tarantula pick its silent way on high hairy legs. At the foot of the black driveway the wild rose hedge had lost its leaves at last. It was winter.

When her mother came out, she jingled the keys to the red roadster in her right hand.

"Mr. Yamaji always walks." Pip said.

Her mother dropped the key ring into her sweater pocket. "Then we will walk. How far is it?"

Pip didn't know. "I got back for lunch," she said.

At first her mother walked too fast and was always ahead

of her. It made her mad having her mother speeding ahead, just like Parkman on the way home from school. When her mother went straight ahead toward the golf course and missed the turn, Pip had to tell her.

"I know how to get there, and you don't," Pip said.

"Oh, I'm sorry, I was gathering my thoughts. I do want to persuade him." Her mother walked more slowly after that.

When they came to the dirt road which led away into the hills, Pip suddenly found that it was unfamiliar. Could it be the right one? She looked up and down the blacktop. Yes, there was the low hill where Mr. Yamaji had waved to her when they parted, and, yes, there were the tracks of her wagon in the soft soil. "This way," she said.

"Are you sure he comes here?" asked her mother. "This is a long way from his house. He lives in another part of the valley altogether."

"I saw him here, Mother." Pip felt anger and impatience with her mother.

She led the way along the dirt road. It was warm between the low hills in spite of the early winter day. Pip pulled her sweater off over her head and wiped her face with it before she tied the sleeves around her waist. At the same instant they reached the place where the valley opened out between the hills, the bleaching white bones appeared.

"What a strange place!" Her mother stood still in the grassy track. "Well, really, Pip, I'm sure you must be mistaken. You've dreamed this, darling."

"I got my bones here!" Pip exclaimed.

[125]

"Well, yes, I know, I'm sure you did. You had to find them somewhere, but about seeing Yamaji — who but you would ever come here, darling?"

Fury flamed up in Pip. Her face burned. She glared at her mother.

"What I mean to say, dearest —"

"Well, he does come here. I know he does. I did not dream it."

"Do you see him?"

"He hasn't come yet, that's all," Pip said. "He sits under the tree right above the last bones. Maybe he's sitting there now." She walked ahead, her heart thumping painfully. No white figure was in sight. Could she be wrong? But Yamaji had said he walked here all the time. People did not always tell her the truth, she had discovered that, not even her mother or Parkman. And sometimes there were meanings she never guessed until someone, usually Parkman, told her. Yamaji might have meant something else. But she didn't see how. Still, as she looked over the bone-strewn valley, she saw no one. He was not under the tree or among the skeletons.

"I think your imagination ran away with you," said her mother.

"It didn't! It didn't," she cried indignantly, wondering if it had. Looking back across the valley, she saw something moving among the bones. "There he is! I knew he'd come, I knew it!"

She wanted to run to him and throw her arms around his waist, and she took three steps before she stopped. Then she walked slowly down the avenue of bones until they met beside the great carcass of ribs she had crawled inside.

"Hello, Mr. Yamaji," She held out her hand.

"Why, hello, Pip. So you have come back again." He took her hand in his brown one and held it for a moment. His face looked a little different from the other times she had seen him. The creases from his nose to his mouth were deeper today, and he seemed tired and thinner, too.

"Are you feeling all right, Mr. Yamaji?"

"You notice so much. I am a little tired, but I am fine now."

"My mother came with me today. She is sitting under the tree."

"We must go and speak to her." Side by side they climbed the wagon ruts to the end of the valley where her mother sat under the twisted live oak tree. She looked suddenly unusually pretty, the dark green sweater over her pale green dress like some protective covering on a spring blossom, and the blue chiffon scarf knotted at her neck like a scrap of sky brought to earth. The sunlight picked out the red-brown shine in her hair.

She held out her hand.

"Hello, Dorrit." Yamaji took her hand as he had taken Pip's and held it a moment. "You wish to speak about Thomas Livingstone."

Looking up at their faces, Pip almost gasped in surprise. Her mother smiled. "Yes, yes, I do, Yamaji."

"Very well. Shall we sit here then?"

Pip squatted on her heels nearby and watched their faces

and hands and their bodies. "He is deeply disturbed," said her mother, and Yamaji said he knew that would be the case. He crossed his knees and laid one wrist over the other. Her mother leaned forward, her thick hair sweeping across her cheeks, and spoke earnestly that Mr. Livingstone was an old man now who had given his life to the cause of world enlightenment and that people all over the world would suffer disappointment and confusion when they heard of the division between the two men.

Pip listened and watched. Yamaji sat in perfect stillness. Even his breathing was undetectable.

When Dorrit had finished, Yamaji said, "For a long time I thought it was impossible to separate from Thomas Livingstone. He has been a father and a teacher and a guide to me. But now I know I must, even at the risk of losing his love and friendship. I shall always love him, but I can no longer do as he wishes me to. Do you see?"

Her mother murmured, "Oh, yes, of course, I see." Then they were silent a long time.

When they rose from the dead log, her mother dusting the back of her dress, Pip stood up, and the three of them walked along the avenue of bones, saying nothing. Pip wandered among the skeletons until she came on a loose rib bone which would finish the skull and crossbones in the corner of her room.

Where the dirt road met the blacktop, they said good-bye. Yamaji held Pip's hand and her mother's hand for a moment before he turned to go up the hill. At the top of the rise he looked back. Pip was waiting to wave when he raised his hand.

After they had walked half the way home, her mother said, "It is entirely clear. He will not be reconciled with Thomas Livingstone. He will not do what others wish him to do."

"He doesn't want to be a chicken." Pip said.

Her mother laughed. "Oh, honestly, darling, you say the funniest things."

Sometimes her mother didn't understand at all.

# ֍ 14 ֎

## Radyar Saves the Day

WHEN THE CHRISTMAS HOLIDAYS BEGAN, the nights and mornings were tinged with frost. Pip lay in bed waiting for the day to warm up and smelled the oily smoke from the smudge pots in the distant orange groves. Finally steeling her nerve, she ran across the icy floor and down the hall to the bathroom where she stood in front of the electric heater until she stopped shivering and the goose bumps on her legs went away. Then she got into her coveralls and sweater which were on the bench where she had left them the night before.

Downstairs a fire leaped in the stone fireplace, and sun streamed in the long windows. The room was warm and smelled of wood smoke and hot cereal and the coffee her mother was sipping on the sofa by the fire.

"What are you going to do today, Pip?"

"I don't know," Pip replied, sitting at the table beneath the window. The cereal was not so good as another Mrs. Huckaby had her try last week. This one had too much oatmeal, she thought.

"Aunt Andrea is coming and we are going to do our yoga exercises, if you want to join us."

"I can stand on my head already."

"That's not all of it, darling," her mother said. "Is Parkman still in bed?"

"He's reading under the covers."

"He'll ruin his eyes."

"He said he'd get up when he finished the chapter, if the floor had warmed up by then."

"He won't get up till April, if he's waiting for that." Pip sat down on the hearth with a slice of lima bean toast and a mug of hot cocoa.

"When's Christmas?" she asked.

"A week from Friday."

"Is Daddy coming from Kansas City?"

"Do you want him to come?"

She couldn't answer for a minute. She did a little, but she didn't, too. She saw the baby doll lying on the track and getting smaller and smaller. He didn't know she had done that. She saw herself riding beside him on the front seat of the big green touring car while he turned the wheel one way then another, never saying anything to her.

"He's not coming. I thought you might be disappointed."

"Who's not coming?" Parkman stood at the bottom of the stairs. He held his thumb between the pages of his book.

"Your father's not coming out for Christmas."

The stillness prickled over Pip as she crouched on the hearth, watching.

"Well, I want him to come!" Parkman cried out. "I want him to come! He came last year!"

"Last year was different," Dorrit said. "Last year was a trial separation. This year is a legal —"

"It isn't different," Parkman exclaimed. "It isn't!"

"I have tried to explain, darling." Their mother got up and carried her coffee tray into the kitchen. Parkman slammed his book against the stone chimney. The paper jacket came loose as it fell. Pip saw the title. *David Goes to Baffin Land.* She wondered if David went there with his father, but she didn't say anything.

Returning, her mother put her arms around Parkman. "Darling, I'm sorry." she said into his hair.

Scowling and rigid, he didn't move.

"Aunt Andy's coming." Parkman seemed to relax a little. "And Christmas Eve Radyar will be here."

Parkman jerked away from her. "Him!" he shouted. "Is he coming?" Savagely he kicked the newspapers across the floor.

"Yes, he is coming!" Dorrit exclaimed. "I am sure Pip is happy about that."

Huddled on the hearth, Pip looked from her mother to Parkman. She wished her mother hadn't said that. In this mood Parkman was a little scary. He rarely showed any anger. When something happened that bothered him, he curled up alone with one of his books. Now he pushed his mother away, picked up *David Goes to Baffin Land* and carefully straightened the jacket. He didn't even look at Pip, and she kept very still. She must stay away from him all day.

That afternoon she walked over to Marjorie Steadman's house, but Marjorie made her mad right off. When she saw Pip at the door, she said, "You can come in, but if you hit me in the stomach, you have to go home." It made Pip feel like giving her a good shove right there. Besides, Marjorie liked to play dolls. All she did was dress and undress them which was a dumb way to spend her time, so Pip left.

Several days passed before she could play with Parkman. Then one day it rained, and the house was damp and cold everywhere except close to the fire or by the electric heater in the bathroom. The bathroom was out because Parkman sat there on the bench reading his new book, *Boy's Life of Colonel Lawrence*, and he didn't come out till it was finished.

Then he came downstairs in a kind of dream and found her in front of the fire and began to tell her the story, how Colonel Lawrence had dressed up like an Arab and had ridden Arabian stallions and been captured by cruel Turks and was smarter than all the British generals in the Near East and had won the World War for them and the Allies. Pip had never read such an exciting book, and neither had Parkman for that matter.

They spent the rest of the day in their striped bathrobes that looked almost like Arab robes and wore bath towels over their heads for headdresses. Parkman had garters to keep up his knee socks, and he gave her one to wear on the bath towel and he wore one, and they looked as much like Arabs as they could manage. Her mother bought a lamb roast which she said Arabs ate, and Mrs. Hernandez baked it with rice and eggplant and tomatoes. They ate squatting by the hearth where the fire still burned and were Arabs as long as they could stay awake. Before she went to sleep, Pip planned to go and live in Arabia as soon as she could. She wondered if they had a landing field for airplanes there.

When Aunt Andrea came to stay, the house rocked with laughter. The telephone bell was ringing and ringing, almost always for her. Somewhere Aunt Andy had lots of friends. Many of them came to see her, men and women in threes and fours and fives, all urging Aunt Andy and her mother to go somewhere and do something like drive to San Francisco to see the sunset on the Golden Gate or go over the mountains to Yosemite and see the snowcap above El Capitan's great stone face. Aunt Andy wore men's pants and shrieked with laughter. Pip couldn't see what was so funny.

The house rocked like a boat in a stormy sea. She never knew when she woke up what she would find. Sometimes it was two strangers in the other beds on the sleeping porch while her mother and Aunt Andy slept in the double bed in the bedroom. One morning people were all over the living room rolled up in quilts, while one man in his underwear shorts sat crosslegged with his eyes closed under the sycamore tree. It was very cold. Pip went into the kitchen where Mrs. Hernandez scowled angrily.

"One more day and I leave," she exclaimed. "They are all crazy people."

They did seem a little crazy. One morning a man called Jack was there when Pip woke up, and after breakfast he gave everyone including her a long scarf and led them out of the house to dance under the oaks. Every so often he called out, "Halt!" and they held very still until he led them on. When he called, "Do as I do," they imitated his movements, and when he shouted, "Express! Express!" they did whatever they felt like doing. Aunt Andy hung by her knees from the sycamore tree, her yellow hair tossing like a mop from her head. The colored scarves waved like flames in the grove.

Parkman stayed in his room and only came out to go to the Saturday matinee with Pip. When they returned, everyone was doing headstands in the living room. Pip hurried fearfully into the kitchen, but Mrs. Hernandez was still there. And she was smiling! Jack in a polo shirt and a butcher's apron stirred a great kettle of soup. Tasting it from a huge spoon, he spoke to Mrs. Hernandez in Spanish. The kitchen smelled very good.

Pip went up to her room and sat down at her desk. The pad of lined paper was in front of her with the words she had written on it:

> *Dear Santa,*
> *I want*

She sat thinking for some minutes before she picked up the thick brown wood pencil and wrote very carefully

> *a helmet*
> *a pair of goggles.*
> > *Love,*
> > > *signed Pip.*

[135]

Early on Christmas Eve day the visitors got in their cars and drove away to Palm Springs, because the desert was more like Bethlehem, and they should be there under the stars as the shepherds had been. They had old blankets for cloaks, and Aunt Andy borrowed Parkman's long underwear to go under her men's trousers.

After they left, the house was very quiet. Pip missed them for a little while. She and Parkman had just settled down before a large bowl of cold popcorn and another of cranberries, and they had threaded large needles with heavy thread and begun to string popcorn and cranberries when she heard a noise on the drive.

"It's Radyar!" she cried. Parkman went on stringing. She jumped up and ran outside. Radyar sat astride his motorcycle, adjusting this and that, and hadn't even taken off his helmet and goggles. Packages stuck out of the sidecar. She helped him carry them to the house.

Her mother didn't want to cut a tree just for a few days inside. It was cruel and wasteful, she said. After lunch they circled the house looking for the right tree outside. They settled for one Parkman picked out, an evergreen which grew outside a long living room window. They could see it from inside. Parkman fastened the colored lights to the branches.

When the popcorn and cranberry chains were ready, they wrapped them round and round the tree. To the ends of the branches they tied suet balls in little string bags for the birds. Radyar secured a silver star to the very top.

That evening they sat around the fire, and Dorrit told the story of Jesus's birth in a little desert town. On the hills shepherds wrapped in coarse woolen cloaks guarded their sheep. "They were Arabs," Parkman said. They were the first ones to see the star which had never appeared in the sky before. "Stars can't do that," Parkman said. "Somebody made that part up."

"It doesn't matter whether it actually happened," Radyar said. "It is a sign of an event of vast importance. The star guided shepherds and kings and marked a certain place. They believed in stars then."

Parkman wound up the Victrola and put on a Christmas carol record. The record was only long enough for one song, and toward the end it ran down. The voice quavering and growing thin set them all laughing. Parkman turned the crank again without lifting the needle, and the voice picked up speed and richness as he wound it up, which made them laugh all the more.

Outside the window the little evergreen glowed red and blue and green and yellow in the dark. When she went to bed, Pip was too sleepy to notice that her letter to Santa was still on her desk.

It took all morning to open the packages. Not that there were so many, but Parkman passed them out one at a time, and they waited while each present was unwrapped and opened and exclaimed over and passed around for everyone to see. Pip waited anxiously. There were baby doll clothes in the box from her father. "Whatever gave him that idea?" asked her mother, and Pip shrugged, fearing Parkman

[137]

would say something, but Parkman was already putting together his new Meccano set and seemed not to hear. A new red sweater lay among the tissue paper in the box from Aunt Andrea. "Don't lose it at the movies, Love, Andy," it said on the card. In one package from her mother was a new pair of blue denim coveralls with red buttons down the front. Parkman gave her a book called *Boy's Story of Lindbergh* which he said was all right for a girl to read. The long tube from Radyar contained her horoscope which when she unrolled it looked like a huge pie with the pieces marked on it. In the margins Radyar had made notes in his small curling handwriting with black India ink. When she saw these, she rolled it up quickly. She couldn't read writing, and she didn't want Radyar to know.

Everyone watched her curiously.

"What's the matter?" Radyar asked, but she couldn't answer.

"Aren't you going to thank Radyar?" asked her mother. Pip bent her head over the wrappings trying to find her coveralls.

"She's afraid she's going to die," Parkman said, looking up from his Meccano set.

"Is that it?" Radyar asked. "There is nothing about death here. It is about guidance for someone of your qualities through a long and successful life."

Suddenly she was weeping into the tissue paper shaken with relief and disappointment.

"Pip! What's the matter?" her mother cried. "It's a day to be happy!"

"I'll bet she didn't get what she wanted," Parkman said.

The tears came in gushes, and her whole body heaved with sobs. Trying to swallow them made her hiccup which hurt her stomach. She shook off her mother's arms and hid her face in some red paper.

"Did you want something special?" her mother asked. Pip nodded. "You didn't send a letter."

She gasped, "I did, too." Then her sobs stopped as she remembered and tried to sit up. "I guess I left it on my desk." She stared at her mother aghast.

Radyar struck his forehead. "Wait a minute now. I should have known." He jumped up and ran out the front door. In a moment he was back, holding both hands behind his back. He took a place on the hearth and faced them across the strewn paper, "I should like to present this gift to the aviatrix of El Dorado Road, Miss Pip dePuyster."

With that he brought his arms forward and held them out to her. In his hands were the extra helmet and goggles from his motorcycle.

"They're yours," Pip said.

"They are yours now," he said.

"But you need them."

"I want you to have them."

Then suddenly she was crying more than ever. She held the helmet and the goggles in both hands and pressed them against her face, but still the tears and sobs would not stop coming.

"What's she crying for now?" Parkman asked.

[139]

"Because she's happy," her mother said.

Sobbing terribly, Pip put her arms around Radyar's waist and held him tight. She felt his hands cradling her head and his fingers press against her curly hair.

# ◙ 15 ◙

## Names

WHEN PIP AWOKE on the sleeping porch the next morning, she sat up immediately in spite of the cold to see if Radyar was still in the extra bed. The covers were thrown back, and the bed was empty. She jumped up, hurried around the end of the beds, and then she caught sight of him below leaning on the sycamore tree, his arms folded on the horizontal limb.

"Radyar," she whispered.

He turned and looked up at the screened porch. "Hurry up," he called, "I'm about to go for a walk." She was into her new coveralls and her gym shoes and her new red sweater which had pockets for her cold hands almost before he had finished speaking.

They struck out across the winter brown grass under the oaks. These oaks stood far apart, but their branches spread out so that one almost touched the next. The bark was heavy and black, the branches were thick and strong and undulating, and the leaves never fell off. Beneath them the thick carpet of grass was wet and cold with dew. Soon Pip's gym shoes were soaked, and her coverall legs flapped heavily. Radyar wore his leather shoes and his leather puttees and didn't notice. Even though her feet were very cold, she didn't mention it. She didn't want to turn back.

They didn't say much until they climbed a hill and came out on the blacktop road. Then he noticed. "You're soaked to the knee, Pip."

"I'm all right." She smiled up at him.

"Come on. We'll go back by the road, and the sun will warm us up."

At each step Radyar's leather heels cracked against the black surface. He took long steps, but somehow she had no trouble keeping up. Ahead of them a flock of shiny blackbirds waddled about looking for something with yellow eyes like kernels of corn stuck in their shiny black heads. Radyar lifted his arms and chanted, " 'Four and twenty black birds, good-bye, good-bye!' " They lifted like springs from the ground and darted away, while she and Radyar laughed. Then Radyar took her hand and said, "That was the army of the black knight, and we have routed them, Squire Pip. Now I think we should partake of some nourishment before we sally forth against the next foe. If we could only find a castle nearby —"

"I know where there's a castle and the cook is very good," Pip said.

Radyar held her hand. "Take me there, Squire Pip."

After that early each morning she and Radyar walked together and met a terrible foe but always won in time to be home for breakfast.

Pip wanted to take Radyar to see the bones and to meet Yamaji, but that morning it rained heavily and a cold fog

settled over the valley. Radyar was as disappointed as she
was.

"I feel that meeting Yamaji would change my life," he
said.

"He has a vision, too," Pip said. "He's looking for thoughts
that are like bones."

Radyar's eyes widened. "Ah," he murmured.

When they had finished breakfast, he said that he wanted
to explain her horoscope to her so that she wouldn't worry
about knowing when she would die. She brought the cardboard tube down from her room, and they spread the great
chart on the floor.

"This is the first horoscope I have cast according to my
new ways of seeing it," Radyar said. "You see, here, Pip,
in the center I have drawn a picture of you. You, an indi-
vidual person, and not a place as in the old ways, are at the
center of the cosmos."

And there at the very center of the chart, Radyar had
drawn a picture of her in her helmet with the goggles on
her forehead. She was smiling and looking up, and little
wisps of hair stuck out of the helmet.

"Each of these sections, the twelve divisions of the year
that look like pieces of pie around the center, have meaning
for you. You are a Leo which is the fifth wedge here which
indicates your basic character and personality and talents. It
simply indicates the best avenues for you to develop. The
position of the sun and the moon and the planets at any one
time tell you when it is the best time for you to do certain
kinds of things and when it is not a good time." Then he

[143]

read to her the written notations he had made in the margins which she could not read because the letters ran together and his handwriting was different from any she had ever seen.

In each wedge Radyar had drawn the little animal or creature which belonged to that segment. Her sign of Leo was a lion. In the corners of the paper he had made other sketches. "These represent the elements," he said. He pointed to the little sketch of her flying an open cockpit plane. "Air," he said. In the opposite corner he showed her diving into the rocky pool: "The element water." He had sketched the sycamore tree in the lower left with just the top of her head showing above the hollow: "You are at home in the earth, too." In the lower right he had drawn an orange and red fire with her seated in front of it looking into the leaping flames: "Fire, the most important element. It tempers us and refines the spirit. When we have experienced fire, then we know."

"But fire hurts."

"I was not thinking of real fire."

Radyar helped her thumbtack her horoscope to her wardrobe door. Afterwards she thought it looked very well there with the Al Wilson pictures all around it and the skull and crossbones nearby.

At night they sat around the fire, and Radyar told stories about Madame Solar in Hollywood. She had black dyed hair and wore great gold hoop gypsy earrings and her real name was Amy Dinkelhoff and she came from Poughkeepsie. She had grown up in a horsehair Victorian parlor, but now she lived in a Persian lair filled with carpets and curtains and incense and strings of beads glittering in the dim light.

Pip fell to thinking about names when she heard this. Her real name was Ann Margaret, but she did not feel like an Ann Margaret. She felt like a Pip. Radyar was Radyar, not Hiram Joseph Smith. Parkman, on the other hand, was Parkman, and no one even thought of calling him Parky or Park. She wondered how he felt inside, if he ever wished he had a nickname, and she glanced toward the black desk chair half in shadow where Parkman sat reading and pretending not to listen. He had the right name to start with. Other people had to find it.

She was reluctant to go upstairs and leave Radyar's stories by the big fire, but Radyar came up to the sleeping porch once she was in bed and they planned where to walk the next day. One night she was so slow to leave that her mother had to ask her over and over until suddenly, his eyes narrow and flashing, Radyar yelled at her, "Get up there!" and she leaped the steps. Shocked and somehow pleased, she lay in bed waiting for him so she could tell him he had hurt her feelings, but he didn't come up.

All the time Radyar was there, Parkman curled up in his chair and read his Christmas books, or he slunk sullenly around and glared at Pip. He scarcely spoke politely to Radyar, and when he had gone, Parkman whispered to her that she was sickening letting Radyar hug her and kiss her and hugging and kissing him. It was disgusting. Pip replied hotly that it was not.

"Pip loves Radyar! Pip loves Radyar!" Jeering, he scraped his finger at her.

"I do not!" she yelled. "I do not!" She tried to hit him, but he leapt away too fast for her. "I do not!" she screamed and ran for her room. She slammed the door so hard that it sprang open, and she could hear Parkman chanting again, "Pip loves Radyar!"

"I do not!" she shrilled and slammed the door all the harder and leaned against it panting with rage. She knew she did, and she hated Parkman for teasing and making fun of what was important and sacred to her.

Then she thought of something. Opening her door a crack, she heard Parkman coming up the stairs jeering. When he took a breath, she yelled, "Mother loves him, too." Parkman stopped as if he had banged into a solid wall. Pip watched a moment before she closed her door, very pleased. Then with a sudden thrill of surprise she wondered if her mother really did.

# ⊜ 16 ⊜

## Illnesses

WHEN SHE GOT BACK to school, Pip's name had risen on the list. Now it was opposite CHECK SUPPLIES, and CHANGE WATER IN TROUGH was next. She felt she had just done this. Soon her name would be opposite CLEAN COOP again, and she looked around for Harold. He wasn't there. He must be home with a cold. Then she remembered that she had not seen him over the holidays, not even at the special matinees. She had been so busy with Radyar that she had forgotten Harold. Now she needed him again, and she hoped his cold would go away soon.

Rain and cold fog hung in the valley. Late one dark Saturday morning she and her mother and Parkman were together before the living room fire. Pip lay on her back on the rug, resting one foot on her raised knee and wiggling her toes to make shadows on the wall opposite the fireplace. Parkman crouched behind the sofa fiddling with the two-box radio. It gave off a terrible crackling as he turned one knob. Suddenly her mother threw down the letter she was reading and exclaimed,

"Where in the world does he get that idea? Honestly, your father has gone cuckoo." She leafed one page behind another. "He thinks Radyar has taken you off to some mountain grotto where you went swimming in the nude."

Suddenly the radio's crackle diminished to a sputter and sizzle like a low fire. Parkman arose from behind the couch and looked at Pip, a silly grin on his face. She tried to shrink into the rug, feeling at the same time that she grew as huge and conspicuous as a hippopotamus. "I didn't have my suit," she whispered.

"How does your father know anything about it?"

"I wrote him a letter." Her voice was just audible.

With a cry her mother threw the letter against the desk's shelf of cubby holes. "Oh, Kansas City! I hate that place! They make everything nasty!" After a moment's thought her mother asked, "And Radyar — did he have his suit?"

"He wore his underwear," Pip whispered. Her lips felt dry and stiff.

"And you — did you keep your underpants on?"

Pip nodded, whispering, "They came off when I dived from a rock, but I got them back on."

"Did you tell him all that?"

Pip thought for a moment. "I just told him we went swimming." Suddenly she sat up and looked at Parkman. Standing behind the couch, he had a funny look on his face. As she stared at him, he sank slowly from sight.

"Oh, Parkman!" her mother cried out. "Oh, Parkman! How could you?"

For a full minute the silence in the room was terrible. Pip felt it pressing against her. Then the electrical crackling from the radio came up louder and louder.

"Parkman!" her mother shouted. "Turn that off!" The room was dead silent again.

After that her mother fell sick with a terrible headache. She lay in the dark bedroom at the head of the stairs, the shutters closed against the light, and scarcely moved in her bed. Whenever Pip came in to see her, she found her mother always lying on her back, her red-brown hair limp and dull against the pillow. It was her mother's worst headache ever.

Mrs. Huckaby came everyday with her basket of electric plates and the little black box. Pip lay on the settee and took a treatment, too, with whatever cold curved metal plates were left over. She lay very still on the little couch, trying to feel the electric current going through her so there would be more of it to help her mother. No matter how hard she tried, she felt nothing, and her mother did not get better. Mrs. Huckaby pursed her lips and shook her head.

"This has never happened before," she said. "It's just a bad one, that's all. I'll be back tomorrow."

After the treatment on the fourth day Pip's mother sat up, asked to have one shutter opened a little, and drank coffee instead of sweet, milky tea. Still her face was tight and very pale, and her eyes were dull so that Pip did not believe she was really very much better.

"She still looks sick," she told Mrs. Hernandez.

"She wants everyone in the world to be happy," Mrs. Hernandez said, "but the world is the way the good God made it. No one can change it."

Thoughtfully, Pip stirred sugar into a bowl of beaten eggs for custard.

"No one can do it, little Pip, not even your mother." Mrs. Hernandez wiped the side of the bowl, and, saddened, Pip licked the spoon.

"Mrs. Hernandez, will you stay with us forever? I want you to."

"I don't know a place any better."

Pip found this a puzzling answer. After they had poured the custard mixture into the baking dish and dusted its top with nutmeg and set it in the oven, she left the kitchen.

When her name came opposite CHANGE WATER, Harold was still not back in school. "Harold is ill," Miss Sixe said, her face growing sad. "They don't know what it is."

A chill passed through Pip. What if he didn't come? She wondered what could be wrong with him that took so long, and she thought of Mrs. Huckaby. With her machine and her health foods and several days to work Mrs. Huckaby could send Harold back to school in time. The day her name went into the slot beside MIX MASH she set out for Mrs. Huckaby's after school.

Mrs. Huckaby was not at home when Pip climbed the driveway and knocked on the rattling screen. Kellogg watched her from the kitchen window, holding out one white paw in mid-lick. Cats never seemed to know you as different and separate, and Kellogg's impersonal stare gave a feeling of strangeness to the rambling house. Pip peered through the glass of the door. Mrs. Huckaby's baskets were gone. She must be out selling her health food.

Pip circled the house and made her way down the hill on the village side, trying to think of places where Mrs. Huckaby might be. The Livingstones' was one possibility. Pip walked two blocks one way and three another to their house behind a row of eucalyptus. Mrs. Livingstone had not seen Mrs. Huckaby lately and asked Pip to have her stop by when she found her.

After that Pip went back to the main street and looked up and down. Bemis the Baker hadn't seen Mrs. Huckaby, and neither had Mr. Steadman the druggist whom she asked while she put a penny in the gum-ball machine by his door. The mailman had met her in the park earlier, but Mrs. Huckaby was not to be seen on the benches under the pergola and along the paths.

Pip left the park by the side street and crossed to the marquee of the Valley Paramount and studied the display windows. Mr. Zick's office door stood open, and after a minute Pip realized that something had changed. No eucalyptus steam billowed through the doorway. When she peeked inside, there was Mr. Zick seated in his swivel chair staring straight ahead. One black metal plate was strapped to his bald head, another was wrapped around each arm, and he held one gently to his chest while another rested across his shoulders. The wires were plugged into the little black box with the dials which was plugged into the wall. Pip went in and stood in front of him so that he needn't move.

"Hello, Mr. Zick," she said. "Do you feel better?"

[151]

"This helps me breathe, Pip. Fifteen minutes everyday and I can breathe like a human being." He wheezed a little when he laughed. "Don't ask me why."

"You sound better," Pip said.

Mr. Zick rolled his eyes. "I am, I am. Back in Brooklyn they wouldn't believe it, and I don't myself."

Pip considered. "I have a friend who is sick. Do you think it will help him?"

"Who knows, Pip? For me it works."

"Is Mrs. Huckaby here?"

"She'll be back to unplug me. Have a seat."

Pip sat down on Mrs. Huckaby's apron where it lay on a straight chair.

"What is on your mind?" asked Mr. Zick.

"Harold is sick."

"Three-fingered Harold? I am sorry to hear that."

He took a deep breath and exhaled. "Do you see that, Pip? No coughing. After twenty years of getting worse, this piece of scrap iron —" he patted the metal plate on his chest "— turns me around." He laughed which brought on a slight cough. "If this thing helps me, it should grow fingers on Harold."

When Mrs. Huckaby came in and Pip explained about Harold, Mrs. Huckaby's face did not brighten in anticipation as Pip expected that it would. Mrs. Huckaby always brightened with anticipation, for some good could always be brought about, but this time her face darkened as Miss Sixe's had. Listening to Pip, she untied the black plates on Mr. Zick's head and arms and replaced them carefully in her basket. Her lips pursed sadly as Pip ran out of words. "I am afraid," she said, bending over her basket, "I am afraid I can do nothing now. They took him to the hospital in Los Angeles this afternoon. I just saw the ambulance go through town. They say he has infantile paralysis."

Although she did not know what infantile paralysis was, Pip felt her heart make two painful thumps like a drumbeat in her chest. She pictured Harold, small and gray and wistful, propped on a great white pillow and looking out the window of the great black and gray ambulance as it rolled by.

Mrs. Huckaby stayed with Mr. Zick to fix his dinner from the jars and boxes of her health foods. Pip walked home alone, knowing that Harold would not be back before her name rose to the top of the list. She saw him growing smaller and smaller as the ambulance disappeared in the distance, and she felt a tug as if string were attached between the ambulance and a rib bone over her heart. Harold needed her.

She pushed open the heavy dark door and entered the house. Parkman was already seated at the dinner table before the porch window, reading in his chair.

"Are you sick or something?" he asked. "You look terrible."

Pip sat down beside him. "Where's Mother?"

"She went to the Livingstones'."

Pip stared out the window above the table. The twisted white branch of the sycamore was all that was visible.

"Parkman."

"What?"

"What's infantile paralysis?"

Parkman dropped his book. "Is that what's the matter with you? Boy, I don't want to be around you then. It's contagious."

"Harold's got it."

"It means your legs don't work. They shrivel up. You know that kid with the silver braces on his legs and the crutches? He had it once. He almost died."

A shivering took over her body, and she had to grip the chair seat for a moment. She saw Harold's legs shriveling to uselessness in the ambulance. He continued to look out the window as death crept over his body. But he couldn't die. No one she knew had ever died. He couldn't. He couldn't. She put her head on the table and wept.

# ⌖ 17 ⌖

## Through Fire

THE CLASS had gathered in its usual early morning semi-circle around Miss Sixe when the lady principal of the school came in followed by a gray-haired man wearing a white coat. A stethoscope hung around his neck. Standing in front of the class the principal smiled a great deal, her lips pulling back and baring her big teeth. There was no reason to be upset, she repeated several times, but the school would be closed until further notice, and if the children would wait patiently in their seats, Dr. Evans would check each of them. Then Dr. Evans said a few words about contagious diseases and explained what Harold had come down with. He called it poliomyelitis, not infantile paralysis, and he wrote it in white chalk on the blackboard. It was longer than Arzoomanian, and it struck Pip as dishonest to have such a long impossible word when they meant that a child's muscles stiffened and shrank and sometimes the child died.

Pip was glad that she had a dress with buttons in front. She didn't have to pull her dress up and show everybody her underpants the way Marjorie Steadman had to. Pip unbuttoned the silver buttons, and Dr. Evans felt across her chest with the cold steel mouth of the stethoscope, while she held the thermometer under her tongue. Barian had a runny nose and was sent into the other part of the L-shaped room. When the doctor was finished, he gave them a sheet of instructions and told them that they must stay at home until they were told to return to school.

Everyone waited for another case of infantile paralysis to develop. Climbing the sycamore tree, Pip let one arm dangle as if it had shriveled up with the disease and she could no longer use it. Parkman had to give her a boost from the rear for her to make it to the crotch of the great branches. Everyday Radyar telephoned from Madame Solar's in Hollywood to ask how they were. Her father called her from Kansas City and she didn't recognize his voice, although Parkman did. No new cases were reported, and all the classes but hers returned. Pip had to abandon her shriveled arm because Parkman wasn't there to boost her. At the beginning of the third week word came from the school that her room could now come back.

It was a relief to Pip, and at the same time her stomach tightened. Her name was now in the slot opposite CLEAN COOP. She refused to think about it. She arrived early and walked up to Mr. Romero's workroom to get the rake. The door was open, and she took the rake and the steel brush. Then she spotted Mr. Romero's clean bandanna handkerchief laid out beside his lunch box. First folding it into a triangle, she put it around her neck, knotted it and then pushed it up over her nose and up the back of her head and over her ears until it stayed up. Then she marched into the chicken coop and raked it clean.

"I had to borrow your bandanna," she told Mr. Romero when he appeared, but he didn't look very upset. "I took you for a bandit," he said, smiling.

As the days went by, Pip became convinced that she could help Harold get well, if she could only see him. He needed her. She didn't know in what way exactly, but in some essential way she was certain.

They would not let her into the hospital, her mother insisted. They would not let her see Harold, but Pip said she didn't care what her mother thought or predicted. She was going to try, and she wept in bitter frustration when her mother said that it was a long trip to Los Angeles and it would be for nothing. She didn't care, she cried, and in the end her mother agreed to drive her there in the red roadster.

Early that Saturday morning she was ready when her mother came downstairs. Wearing her embroidered blue dress and her Christmas sweater, she waited, her helmet and goggles beside her. Once they were seated on the yellow-brown seats of the red roadster, she pulled on the helmet, pushed the last wisps of hair under the edge and set the goggles, one round glass eyepiece carefully over each eye. "Contact, let 'er go," she said.

Her mother roared the engine with the accelerator before she grasped the round knob on the gearshift between them and set the stick into first gear. The roadster moved down the drive.

The blacktop road stretched straight as a string through the village and the deep shiny green orange groves beyond it to the upper end of the valley. Then it cut back and forth, each turn taking it higher, as it climbed over the mountains which held the valley like a cup. At the top of the grade there was a break in the twisted live oak trees, and through it as they passed, Pip could see the length of the entire valley — the orange groves, the roofs of the village, the thick oaks covering the place where their house stood, the brown foothills and the far high rim of mountains. Then the roadster turned its back on the view and sped through high meadows where cattle grazed. As they drove, her mother said, "I didn't know you liked Harold so much."

Pip stared straight ahead through her goggles. It was not a matter of her liking Harold a whole lot. She liked him enough, even when, sitting next to her, he let his head settle against her shoulder and she had to hump it up to push him away. Something else bound her to him. She had no words for it and sat in silence behind her goggles as the roadster plunged into the narrow twisting canyons which an hour later disgorged the little red car on the plain around Los Angeles.

Tall palm trees lined the drive which curved toward the great white hospital. Her mother parked the car opposite the flight of white steps, and Pip flew up them. Standing before the great counter in the hospital lobby, she said, "I want to see Harold."

"Harold who?" asked the woman in pinched-nose glasses.

"Harold Hoffer," she said.

The woman ruffled through the files and returned shaking her head. "I am afraid," she said, "he cannot have visitors. No one is allowed to see him. He is in isolation."

"How sick is he?" Pip asked, but the woman didn't know, asking if she would like to write him a note.

Pip sat down at a table and wrote on a piece of hospital stationery:

> *Dear Harold*
> *I came to see you.*
> *I cleaned the coop myself.*
> *I hope you feel better.*
> *Love*
>
> *Pip*

The woman behind the desk took it and said she would see that Harold received it.

Afterwards Pip and her mother ate lunch in silence in a Pig'N'Whistle. At the end her mother said, "What shall we do with this empty afternoon?" She herself would like to see the new cars at the automobile show. Pip didn't care one way or the other. Her mother drove about until she found the great spreading tent where the show was held. Parking the roadster on a side street, they followed a throng of people going toward the entrance. Her mother took her hand as they hurried along, squeezed it and began to smile. Immediately excitement and interest rose in Pip.

The great tent was bright inside. Her feet scuffed through thick sawdust. Young women in beautiful clothes with tossing yellow hair like Aunt Andy's were everywhere around the shining new automobiles. On a raised platform opposite the entrance stood a gleaming white Duesenberg. Its magnificence took her breath.

"Pip darling, do you need to go to the ladies' room?" She shook her head. "I do. You wait for me right here by this car, will you, darling? I'll be right back."

Pip touched the shining spokes of the wheels and smelled the clean new rubber of the black tires. It was an open car with the tan canvas top folded back, and the red leather seats smooth and springy. A girl in a short skirt and shining silk stockings tossed wild yellow curls and leaned back against the front fender, lifting her shoulder to her chin while a man popped in and out of a black cloth which was thrown over a camera box. Pip wondered if they were in the movies and if they knew Al Wilson, the great Daredevil of the Sky.

Standing still watching them, she didn't hear someone shouting until the girl straightened up suddenly, her shoulder dropping, and she began to scream. The man grabbed her arm, and they looked wildly around. A crowd rushed toward them.

"Fire!" Everyone was yelling and screaming and running. "Fire! Fire!"

"My mother!" Pip cried. She dashed head on into the crowd.

"Grab that kid!" a man shouted. "Get her out of here. Fire! Fire! In the ladies' room. Somebody dropped a cigarette in the sawdust. Out under the back flap!"

"Mother!" Pip screamed and dived between the onrushing legs. "Mother!"

"Catch that kid. Don't let her go that way!"

"But my mother's in there," Pip screamed. She wrenched away from the clutching hands. "Let me go! Let me go!"

The crowd was dense and coming toward her. She struggled against it, pushing and shoving, digging her feet into the slippery sawdust. Then suddenly arms embraced her. "Pip! Oh, thank God, I've found you!" Her mother gripped her hand. "Come, this way. The entrance is this way."

"No, Mother. This way." Pip pulled her mother away from the pressing crowd. "Out under the back flap!"

Hand in hand they ran among the automobiles, along the sawdust paths, away from the crowd. Everyone was pressing toward the entrance, pushing and shoving, trying to get through. The back way was clear. Her mother lifted the flap of the tent, and they scrambled under. They found themselves in a tiny yard blocked by a six-foot high fence.

Her mother whispered, "Oh my God!"

The tent was behind them. They could hear the crowd screaming and now they smelled the smoke.

"Pip, I'll boost you up, and you climb over and drop down on the other side."

"I won't without you!"

"You must! You have to! I'll get over. I'll make it somehow. Here—" She took off her pointed shoes and threw them over the fence. Then she threw her pocketbook over. Gripping Pip around the thighs, she lifted her until Pip's fingers curled over the boards. With a boost on her bottom Pip dug her toes against the fence and swung one leg over the top.

At that moment a man ducked under the tent flap and took a flying leap for the top of the fence. Pip gripped the fence hard with both knees and shoved the man back.

"Help my mother over the fence!" she screamed.

The man picked himself up from the dirt, cursing wildly, grabbed her mother and shoved her upward to the top of the fence. Dorrit dug her toes against the boards, swung over the top, and with Pip, dropped to the ground. The man was already streaking toward the street.

Pip found one shoe and the pocketbook, her mother the other shoe, and hand in hand they ran between the apartment buildings to the street.

The air was filled with sirens and smoke and distant shouting. Two firemen in rubber coats carrying axes and an extinguisher between them ran toward the fence. "Get away from here, lady, we don't know what will go up." The sky was dark gray like a late rainy afternoon.

"I have to go to the bathroom," Pip panted.

Her mother found a corner of thick shrubbery and stood guard. Afterwards they walked to the wide street where the entrance to the tent had been. The way was choked with fire engines. Hoses like snakes crisscrossed the street. Big men in black rubber coats held the shining nozzles as they squirted great arcs of water into the tent.

They crossed the street and made their way along the edge. There were no flames to be seen. It was all smoke and steam hissing like a tea kettle and the great arcs of water catching the light.

"I hope everyone got out safely," her mother said. They walked on.

"Did you see the fire in the ladies' room?" Pip asked.

"No, I never got there. I was almost there when the women came running out, screaming fire, and I turned around right away."

"A man said a cigarette fell in the sawdust."

"It could have. It may be true. Oh, Pip, we were lucky! Lucky again!"

They climbed into the roadster, and her mother sat back behind the wheel for a few minutes. "I think we should have a cup of tea before we start for home."

Pip said, "I'm hungry and I have to go to the bathroom again."

"It's the excitement," said her mother. "We'll find a restaurant with a rest room." She started the motor and pulled away from the curb. "What a shame. That was such a beautiful Duesenberg."

Pip sighed. "I wanted to see them all."

"Do you like cars better than aeroplanes?"

Pip shook her head. "Cars don't have wings." And her mother smiled. "Of course, I should have known that."

The late winter afternoon was fast disappearing before the red roadster emerged from the canyons leaving Los Angeles. Twilight gathered as it sped across the high mountain meadows. Pip peered into the darkness to see if the cattle still grazed beside the road, and as she studied the open pastures, a feeling took shape in her head. Suddenly she spoke out loud, "Mother, I think Harold is going to be all right."

Her mother cast her a sideways glance. "What makes you think that out of the blue?" she asked, but Pip returned to her study of the meadows and didn't reply. She didn't know how she knew, but in some secret place within her she knew. Harold would be all right.

# ☙ 18 ❧

## New Developments

MARJORIE STEADMAN squealed as her hands broke through the thin ice on the water trough. It sickened Pip to hear her. She suspected that she shrieked to attract Barian's attention. He was still in Mr. Romero's workroom, mixing the mash. The first drift of its smell had just come past her.

Mr. Romero tied his bandanna handkerchief over Pip's nose and mouth. The thick square knot pressed into the back of her head. Then she took the brush with the steel bristles and the fine-toothed rake, entered the coop and went straight to the hen house.

The hen house was small, and the smallness made it worse. When the boys and Mr. Romero built it, they had not thought about windows. After all, a chicken didn't need to see out. But a hen house needed air which came only through the open doorway. The sun beat down on the flat tarpaper roof making the inside an oven for baking chicken droppings. On three sides of the house they had built a shelf like a shallow window box which was stuffed with straw. If they ever laid an egg, the chickens were supposed to do it in the straw nests. There was only one hen left in the house

[165]

when Pip entered, and it squawked from its perch and flapped its big white wings. When it hopped on the edge of the shelf, Pip ducked and covered her head with her hands. The hen flapped past her so closely that one wing struck the top of her head.

"Dummy," Pip muttered, propping the rake against the wall. She tried to hold her breath, but it was impossible. Brushing the sides of the shelf to loosen all the crusted droppings took too long. She drew little short gasps through her lips which already moistened the bandanna where it covered them.

When she had scraped down the shelf, she raked the floor. The smallness of the house made this difficult, too. The end of the rake continuously cracked against one wall or another, making it impossible to take long sweeps and work fast. She raked everything into a pile by the door.

The yard was much easier, because she could make long pulls on the rake. When she had made a second pile by the chicken-wire gate, she went out and brought back the wheelbarrow from Mr. Romero's workroom and shoveled the two piles into the barrow. Looking back over her work, she rather liked the looks of it. The yard was crisscrossed with rake tracks. Where she crossed with the barrow, she raked again. Only one lone hen tiptoed across the pattern, leaving three pronged prints in the raked dust.

"You forget clean straw," Mr. Romero said.

"What?"

She had forgotten to remove the old straw from the shelf. She looked up at Mr. Romero.

"Never mind. I do it for you."

"It's my job," Pip said, pulling the bandanna over her nose and mouth again.

"That's all right. I finish up," he smiled.

"No!" Pip shook her head, surprised that she spoke so firmly. Pushing the wheelbarrow ahead of her, she crossed the coop again.

She had to leave the barrow at the doorway as it was too big to go through. Inside the same dumb hen had returned to its nest. Pip waved her arms and yelled, "Move, dummy!" and then she ducked. The chicken hopped to the edge, squawked and flew past her again. Pip crossed to the shelf, and then she saw it.

A beautiful white egg nestled in the dirty straw. Pip went over to it and looked. Yes, it truly was an egg, the very first to be laid. She touched it with her finger tip. It was warm. She closed her hand around it. The shell seemed to grow stronger in her grasp.

"Well!" she whispered. She pulled down the bandanna and turned the knot around to the front where she could work on it. When she loosened it, she folded the handkerchief in the palm of her hand and made a carrying nest for the egg. Cradling it gently, she left the hen house.

"What you have there?" cried Mr. Romero as she passed, but she didn't stop. Marjorie Steadman hippety-hopped along, squealing, "Show it to me, Pip. Show it to me first." Barian broke into an unbelieving grin. She mounted the two steps to the classroom, marched to the front, followed by Mr. Romero and Marjorie and Barian, and stood in front of Miss Sixe where she sat on a little chair among the children.

"Look," Pip said and held up her cupped hands.

"Oh, for heaven's sake!" cried Miss Sixe. "It happened!"

The others jumped up from their chairs and crowded so closely, shrieking "Let me see!" and "I want to see!" until Pip yelled, "Stay back! You're going to make me drop it!"

"Let's get this in a box on the windowsill," said the teacher. "We don't want to lose our very first egg."

Miss Sixe took a yellow Crayola box and cut it in half. Pip laid the bandanna on the bottom with the smooth white egg on top. It sat on the windowsill all day. After the excitement was over, only then did she remember that she hadn't changed the straw. Now that eggs were coming, it would be important to have clean straw. What's more, she had left the wheelbarrow standing at the doorway. When she went back at recess, the wheelbarrow was gone and the straw was clean. Mr. Romero sat smoking on the threshold to his workroom.

"Thank you, Mr. Romero," she said.

"Don't mention," he said.

"I didn't mean to forget."

"So now these chickens make themselves useful," he said. "That is good."

That afternoon Pip wrote a letter to Harold and told him about the egg. She decorated her letter with little drawings. By the time school was out there were two more eggs in the straw. The next day one more. By the end of the week most of the hens were laying one egg everyday. The people in the cafeteria were very pleased and bought them all.

After that everyone wanted the job of changing the straw. Even though the shelf had to be scraped clean, it was exciting to paw through the straw first to find all the eggs. In the middle of the second week of laying, Marjorie Steadman tried to grab an egg before Barian got it and broke it open right on the shelf. Dismayed, they watched the sticky clear stuff and the broken yellow center spreading across the dirty board.

"It doesn't have a chicken in it," Marjorie said.

Barian watched the egg drop through a crack. "Of course not. We don't have a rooster."

"Why do you have to have a rooster?" Marjorie asked, and Barian said, "You just have to, that's all."

When the class had pulled up their chairs in the semicircle around Miss Sixe, Pip asked, "If we had a rooster, could we have baby chicks?"

Miss Sixe looked a little startled at first, but after a moment she said, "Now that is an idea." When she had thought a little longer, she added, "Well, Pip, you are chairman of the chicken committee. Will you please talk to Mr. Arzoomanian and tell him we would like a rooster. We can pay for it with our egg money. Marjorie, how much money do we have now?"

By the time Marjorie added it all up, their heads were bent in silent reading. The sum was exactly five dollars and forty-two cents.

Although her head, too, was bent, Pip did not read. She

examined each page of the reader, then turned it, looking for any mention of a rooster. There was none in the chicken story they had read last fall, and as far as she could detect, there was no rooster story nor did a rooster appear anywhere. When she turned the last page, she sat back, feeling pleased. Marjorie had made Barian think of a rooster, and she had asked Miss Sixe, and Miss Sixe had agreed to getting one. This time no one had been tricked. She would ask her mother to take her immediately to Arzoomanian's Egg Ranch.

When Mr. Arzoomanian emerged from the long hen house, his bib overalls were dirty, and his belly strained them tighter than ever. Under them he wore an old white dress shirt with the button-on collar missing. While he listened to Pip's story, he thrust a pipe under his great moustache and lit it, puffing quickly over and over while the match flared.

"What did I tell you?" he said. "Those White Leghorns are good laying hens. For eggs take the White Leghorns. Remember I said that?"

"You said they were machines for making eggs," Pip said, and it still offended her. To live your whole life as a machine was a condition she could not see as good. Still eggs were eggs, and they were useful. "Nine of the hens lay an egg everyday," she told him.

"Seventy-five percent! You are taking care of them right. So now you want a rooster to get some chicks in those eggs?" He puffed rapidly. "I think I got two-three Leghorn roosters. You can take your pick." He led the way around the long white hen house to a cluster of open chicken-wire runs with a rooster in each one.

Pip squatted by the first run and looked through the wire at its occupant. The White Leghorn rooster raised one yellow claw and stared stupidly back at her. He looked like the hens, only he was bigger with a fuller chest and longer legs and neck. The real difference was his great red, comb which grew from the top of his head and the great red, wrinkly-skinned wattle hanging from his chin. They offended her.

The other two runs held roosters just like him. Beyond them was another run, and in it Pip saw a great red-brown rooster with black tail feathers arcing to the ground behind him. His comb was black, and his eyes were black, not stupidly red. Pip said, "Mr. Arzoomanian, I want that one."

"That's a Rhode Island Red. You want a White Leghorn to go with your hens."

"Will that hurt the chicks?" she asked.

"No, you get chicks all the same. I don't know what they will look like, but —"

"Then I want that one."

"Well, it don't matter to him what hens you got." Mr. Arzoomanian gave a great guffaw.

"How much does he cost?"

"Five dollars for that one. Four-fifty for the Leghorn."

"I have five dollars. Will you please wrap him up?"

Mr. Arzoomanian guffawed again. "I'd better put him in a box for you." He opened the run and with one great sweep of his arm he caught the rooster by the feet and pulled him out. The rooster squawked angrily, but he was held fast in the great paw. Hanging upside down, he craned his neck upwards and looked at Pip as she followed Mr. Arzoomanian to his little office. There he put the rooster in an old box and cut holes in it for air, and she counted out five dollars from the money in her sweater pocket.

Pip was pleased all the way home. When her mother drove the red roadster up the driveway and they saw Radyar's motorcycle standing under the great oak, she was even happier.

"Did you know he was coming?" asked her mother, but Pip shook her head. "That's curious. He always calls before he comes."

In the living room Radyar was seated on the sofa. Opposite him Parkman sat in the armchair and fiddled with the corduroy of his knickers where it bagged over his knee. Pip paid no attention and ran to Radyar. In one swift glance she saw that Radyar was not his usual neat self. His hair sprang back from his forehead instead of being slicked down like Rudolph Valentino's. He wore a four-button sweater with slashes of grease on the sleeve. His riding pants were rumpled, and his puttees and boots covered with dust. Hugging him, she felt electric tension in his body. Something was wrong, she knew it. When her mother spoke, her voice warmed the whole room.

"Radyar! What has happened?"

"I have broken with Madame Solar," Radyar said.

Pip felt a great joy rising inside her as her mother said, "Oh, Radyar, I am so glad."

"I hoped you'd say that. I wanted someone to say that. I have been through hell." He broke into a short laugh, and his eyes flashed. "But I could not write those meaningless little squibs one more day."

Joy spread through Pip.

"How I am going to eat I don't know, but that will take care of itself."

"Of course it will," her mother said. "Pip, tell Mrs. Hernandez there will be one more for dinner."

Through dinner and afterwards Radyar talked, telling them what happened with Madame Solar. How her dyed black curls had trembled when he told her he felt like a liar every time he wrote her column. Her black eyes had narrowed until they gleamed like the edge of a knife blade through her black dyed lashes. She had screamed like a clawed animal when he disagreed with her reading of the planets. They had battled all day without stopping to eat or drink or even catch breath. At midnight he had stomped out with Madame Solar shrieking behind him. All night he had turned and tossed and paced his room seething with the battle and his fears and convictions. At eight in the morning his telephone rang. It was Madame Solar, her low voice thrilling with reason. Something, she was sure, could be arranged. He had gone back to her Persian lair, and in ten minutes she was enraged and snatched a letter opener from her desk and came at him. "I fled for my life," Radyar said. He had gone home where he fell into an exhausted sleep. At six Madame Solar called again, and again she was cool and reasonable, and again he had gone back. She had prepared him a great dinner and through the meal they talked business. Surely they could work together. After all she was not so young anymore. There were bound to be new ways of interpreting the data, but it was helping people that mattered. And the money — "You have to eat, you know," Madame Solar said, giving him more eggplant. Still they could not agree. Madame Solar had lost the vision long ago and had settled for telling fortunes for money. They battled again. At midnight Madame Solar sank exhausted on her Persian carpeted divan and threw her arm over her black eyes and said that she couldn't stand anymore. "When you are hungry," she had cried, "you will come back."

For hours Radyar rode his motorcycle up and down the highways not knowing where he went until late in the afternoon he found himself in the valley.

"I hope by my lucky stars that I am never that hungry," he said.

"There is no reason why you should be," Pip's mother said. "I have quite an ample supply of money."

Radyar sat up suddenly on the couch. "Dorrit, I cannot do that. I did not come here to — to play on your sympathies."

"I should be happy to help you."

Radyar laughed, taking her hand, "My dear beautiful Dorrit, marrying you would be quite a help, I would say."

She freed her hand to take his. "I was not thinking of marriage. I was thinking of some kind of gift."

"Dorrit, I could not — I could not accept your money."

"Oh, it isn't mine really. It comes from the wheat of Kansas, and I don't know why it shouldn't help you with your work and give you time to develop your own vision."

Smiling, Radyar looked at Pip and spread his arms wide. "The golden wheat of Kansas! What bounty! I feast at this table." He fell back against the sofa with a sigh.

It was midnight. In her corner of the sofa Pip pressed her head into the loose pillow. Her eyelids ached from holding them up. Even Parkman had stayed to listen, sitting stiffly upright on the black desk chair at the edge of the little group. They were silent for several minutes as the clock chimed twelve.

Then Radyar exclaimed, "Oh, this beautiful valley! Here among the mountains we are free to discover our true spirits. We have our chance to try our wings." He took Pip's hand in his. Pip felt her whole body swollen and tight with love. It filled her like a balloon. She felt a connection with Radyar, but it was not a string like the one connecting her with Harold. It was more like the recognition which must pass between two aviators just before going into a loop-the-loop.

The next morning Radyar took her to school on his motorcycle. Sitting in the sidecar she held the box with the rooster in it on her lap.

"Well, it's a beautiful rooster," Miss Sixe said, "but it doesn't match our hens."

"It doesn't matter to the rooster," Pip said. "Mr. Arzoomanian said so."

"Hmmm, I see," said Miss Sixe. "I wonder what the chicks will look like with a Rhode Island Red father and a White Leghorn mother. Did he say?"

"He doesn't know."

"Well, I suppose we can think of it as a scientific experiment."

The class stirred with doubt and interest. They agreed it was a beautiful rooster which at the moment seemed more important than what the chicks might look like when they appeared in the distant future.

# 🐚 19 🐚

## Yamaji under the Oaks

RADYAR MOVED into the one-room house behind the Livingstones', and Pip helped him settle his belongings. His canvas bag of clothes and five cardboard cartons of books and charts and a large maple-topped drawing table that set on a slant had somehow been stowed into the rumble seat of her mother's red roadster which she had loaned to Radyar to move from Los Angeles. He told Pip where to put his books on the shelves and how to stack his chart-making materials beside the drawing board. The room had a wide window seat with a mattress for a bed, and shelves to the ceiling and one large window which gave a view of the bare rock-face high in the mountain ridge which she had pointed out to him the afternoon of their first ride into the foothills. When he had put away his clothes, he had moved in.

The almond trees in the upper valley burst into bloom, and pale pink flowers covered the small trees in grove after grove. The sweet, sharp scent drifted everywhere on the breeze.

About the time the almond petals had fallen, word came about Harold. He still lay in the distant hospital, but he had improved. One leg was all right. The doctors planned to operate on the other leg and remove the muscle on the inside of his thigh. Pip found herself clutching her leg tight in both hands when Miss Sixe told them this. What would it be like, she wondered, to have only part of your leg left? Could you walk or run or climb or swim ever again? And then always people would stare at your funny leg. It seemed a dirty trick on Harold who already had his three-fingered hand. Miss Sixe said the operation was a common treatment for infantile paralysis. The doctors cut away the shriveled muscles, making the leg sometimes quite all right. Still Pip hoped that this would not happen to Harold, who had, she felt, had enough.

After the almonds the orange trees broke into bloom. Huge round oranges still hung on the trees while the wax-like white flowers burst into little trumpets from every twig. Their fragrance was strong and heavy and filled the valley day and night like an invisible smoke. Pip thought they looked like artificial trees with their shiny dark green leaves and the waxy white flowers and the perfect round oranges which reminded her of the round yellow lights some people used on their Christmas trees.

It wasn't long before Mrs. Huckaby put Radyar on her list of customers. On a Saturday morning Pip coasted as far up Mrs. Huckaby's drive as her wagon would go and helped her stow her basket of health foods in the wagon bed. Between them they pulled the wagon into the village to visit Mrs. Huckaby's customers. When she stopped at the Living-stones', Mrs. Huckaby went around in back to make a sale to Radyar. She pressed a box of vegetized crackers and a jar of malted nuts on him. Pip told him they were delicious, and he agreed to give them a try.

"You need a hot plate," said Mrs. Huckaby, "so you can cook up some greens and a good soup. I can get you one from Mr. Zick. He doesn't use it anymore now his asthma is better." When Radyar protested that he didn't want to do his own cooking, she brushed that aside. "It's better than cheap cafés, terrible places. They'll do you in." Pip wondered where these cheap cafés were that Mrs. Huckaby talked about. There were no restaurants in the village. The sweet shop had only ice cream and sandwiches, and the ice cream was delicious.

"It's cheaper, too," Mrs. Huckaby said, "to do your own cooking."

But Radyar scowled and said, "Please don't, if you don't mind, Mrs. Huckaby. I don't want to spill soup on the ancient texts or plop a forkful of spinach on a valuable horoscope. Mr. Zick's asthma may come back any day so he'd better keep his hot plate."

"Well, he's a deep one," Mrs. Huckaby said when they left. "I was just trying to help."

"He's a Scorpio," Pip said.

"And there's a bit of the scorpion in him, too. All innocent looking but still with the sting in the tail when they want to use it."

In Mrs. Huckaby's bathtub the three scorpions still plodded through the dust which was now deeper and dustier. In her head Pip saw one crawling about wearing the face of Radyar and another with the face of Madame Solar as she imagined that face fringed with quaking black curls. Pulling the wagon, Mrs. Huckaby said, "You never sell anything making an argument, Pip, remember that."

"I will, Mrs. Huckaby," she said.

The next time she stopped in at Radyar's, he had a hot plate, and he boiled water on it and made two cups of tea, one for him and one for her, putting lots of milk and sugar in hers. Radyar sat crosslegged on the window-seat bed, and she sat at his drawing board which he had set flat for her to rest her cup. They ate vegetized crackers, and after a while Radyar asked, "Pip, have you ever been to the air circus?"

She shook her head.

"Do you know what an air circus is?"

"Al Wilson, the Daredevil of the Sky, is in them all the time. I've seen them at the matinee on Saturdays."

"Would you like to go to a real one?"

She stared at him while her lungs contracted. "A real one?"

"There's going to be a big air show in San Diego the first of June. I'd like to see it myself. All the barnstormers will be there, buzzing the rooftops, spiraling, nose dives, barrel rolls, loop-the-loops. Acrobatics in the air. Men riding the wings doing tricks. Would you like to go and see it for yourself?"

Pip could not speak. Blood flooding into her head filled it to bursting.

Radyar smiled. "So you would like to go. I thought you would. An aviatrix will be there. She's very famous, and she's going to do stunts in the air. I am casting her horoscope now. She is a good friend, and I want you to meet her."

To come face to face with a real aviatrix, to take her hand, to see what kind of goggles and helmet and scarf she wore, to see her climb into the cockpit and make the sign to the contacts to pull out the blocks from the wheels under her plane, to be right there while someone spun the propeller and the real aviatrix guided the little canvas-covered plane out into the open field until it pointed in the same direction as the fluttering wind sock, to watch her speed ahead and pull back the joystick to lift the little plane from the ground into the air — Pip saw it all so clearly. Then, once the real aviatrix had her plane in the air, she would turn and come back against the wind and leaning out of the cockpit she might look straight at Pip and give the salute. Clutching Radyar's chair, Pip could not for a moment get her breath.

"Well, I rather thought you'd like to go," Radyar said. "It will have to be an overnight trip. We will talk to Dorrit about it."

When she heard about it, her mother cried, "We will all go. We'll take the roadster. Pip and Parkman love to ride in the rumble seat."

That evening Pip made a large calendar so she could mark off the days until June first.

Just as the fragrance of orange bloom filled the valley, so their house began to fill with people. Aunt Andrea arrived with the dancer Jack who had stayed there before Christmas. With them was a woman dancer whom they called

Ruth-darling, and Pip had never seen anyone like her. She was extraordinarily slender and strong like steel, and she walked as if her body hung from her neck and her head was suspended in air rather than being held up. When Pip arose early in the morning, Ruth-darling was already outside on the terrace doing her exercises with one hand resting lightly on the horizontal sycamore limb. One morning Pip found her dancing among the oaks and asked her what she was doing, and she said she was making up a dance to go with Yamaji's poem, "Finding the Way."

Sitting at the porch table drinking her hot chocolate and eating the lima bean toast Pip wondered what it meant, and she watched Ruth-darling carefully as she bent her back over the sycamore limb and then ran, her thin arms trailing like vines, among the oaks.

More people came and sat crosslegged with their eyes closed while others stood on their heads for minutes on end. People appeared from as far away as Chicago and England, because Yamaji was going to talk in the park under the great oaks. Pip heard their visitors speak in awe of Yamaji as the great man and the great teacher, and she imagined that he would look different from the way he did when they had walked together among the bones. He must have grown bigger, she thought, and she saw everyone gathered in a semicircle around him, each sitting on a little yellow oak chair.

When the day came, there was unusual quiet in the house. The guests did not say very much to each other, and so Pip was quiet, too. She felt that something tied them together as they walked in a little group down the road into the village. Parkman carried a blanket for them to sit on, and so did Jack the dancer.

Other people in groups and in pairs and one by one crossed the main street by the post office and entered the village park. It was not a park which had been planted but a portion of an oak grove which had been left alone in the heart of the village. Paths had been worn through the grass and a few benches set along them. At the far side the land sloped downward making a natural amphitheater. People were already there under the oaks.

Her mother and Parkman spread out the blanket. Next to them Jack opened his for Aunt Andrea and Ruth-darling. They were no sooner settled than Radyar appeared, and the three of them made room for him on their blanket. Although the crowd grew bigger and bigger, it was quiet under the trees. Then as the bell in the post office struck its dull-toned eleven o'clock, Yamaji appeared.

He stood quietly between two oaks and waited. He wore his usual white shirt and white trousers, and his dark face was pleasant. He was no bigger than he had been before, and he looked no different. Even his voice was unchanged, not even louder than she had known it. Waiting, his dark eyes traveled over the audience, and when he saw her seated on the blanket before him, he smiled a little and began, "We have come here to be together." There was a long pause. "— to talk together in our search for the way of truth." He waited again. "If you have come to have me tell you how to find the way, you may as well fold your blanket now and depart. Not this speaker — nor any other speaker — can give you precise directions for finding the way."

After these words he waited a long time. Pip saw Mr. Livingstone seated on his cane under an oak. He wore his usual gray suit and his wide-brimmed Panama hat. Mrs. Livingstone sat beside him in a folding chair. They listened as attentively as the others and did not look in the least angry with Yamaji.

"Each of us must find the way which is his own," Yamaji said, and then he repeated it. "Each of us must find the way which is his own. That is the point from which we must begin."

Beside her Radyar nodded as he listened. Pip felt a warmth like a small fire in the bottom of her lungs.

She did not understand what Yamaji went on to say, and the words did not stay in her mind. Standing very still he talked until the deep bell in the post office tower struck twelve o'clock. He stopped when it began to ring and waited. For a few minutes there in the sun and deep oak shade and the stillness of all the people, the air trembled with sound. When the bell stopped, Yamaji turned and walked away.

They sat on their blanket for some minutes after Yamaji had gone. Around them others waited, too. Mr. Livingstone remained seated on his sporting cane under the oak, and after a while two people went up to speak with him. Finally, her mother and then Radyar got up, and Pip and Parkman folded the blanket which Parkman carried. Jack and Aunt

Andrea and Ruth-darling got up, too. Then they gathered around the Livingstones, and together they walked away through the park.

Pip was never to forget that day nor Yamaji's words nor the feeling of fire inside her nor the quietness of everyone around her as if they were occupied deep within themselves. Nor would she forget the touch of Radyar's hand around hers as they left the park.

There was a great picnic that day behind their house. Mrs. Huckaby came with platters of nut loaf and bowls of black Savita gravy which she kept separate so Parkman would try the loaf, and she made Mr. Zick sit down and not do anything in case he brought his asthma back. There were all kinds of vegetables and fruits including oranges and strawberries dusted with powdered sugar and fresh coconut which Pip particularly liked and a great kettle of thick soup and more fresh lima bean buns than she had ever seen before outside the bakery itself. They sat on the grass around the sycamore tree and ate quietly. It surprised Pip that Yamaji didn't come, and she asked Mr. Livingstone why he was not there.

"He is more and more alone," said Mr. Livingstone.

"He would not be alone if he had stayed with you," Mrs. Livingstone said, but her husband held up his hand to silence her. "No, no, he must go his own way."

In her head Pip saw the solitary white figure standing among the bones, and she felt a surge of loneliness and sadness and then again the intense feeling of fire.

[185]

The house was so filled with people and activity that no one noticed the yellow telegram lying on the black desk. A messenger had delivered it while they listened to Yamaji under the oaks, and Mrs. Hernandez had laid it there.

# ◙ 20 ◙

## Telegrams from Kansas City

PIP DID NOT LIKE the color yellow, and when she saw the half sheet of coarse yellow paper in her mother's hand, she sensed that it was ominous. Her mother held it in front of her as she read and let her hand fall to her side as she finished. "I cannot believe it," she said. She lifted the paper and read it again. This time when she finished, she turned to Pip and said, "It is from your father."

"Is it bad?" Pip knew it was.

"You will be disappointed, I fear."

"Is it about me?" She knew that it was bad news from the yellow and the way her mother held it and the expression on her face and the tenseness of her body, but she had not realized that it had to do with her.

Her mother lifted the yellow sheet again and read aloud:

I FORBID REPEAT FORBID YOU TO ALLOW PIP TO ACCOMPANY THE MAN RADYAR ANYWHERE REPEAT ANYWHERE STOP I QUESTION YOUR COMPETENCE AS MOTHER TO PERMIT MAN OF QUESTIONABLE CHAR-ACTER NEAR CHILDREN STOP IF YOU PERSIST I SHALL TAKE LEGAL ACTION STOP

EDWARD DEPUYSTER

[187]

Pip sat down as if she had been hit in the stomach. "But Radyar's taking me to the air circus!" she cried.

"Don't worry," said her mother. "Your father doesn't understand. I shall explain everything to him. I am sure it will be all right."

But Pip was filled with dread. There were things her mother didn't understand, and if she didn't, the silent, distant man who was her father never would. He didn't understand her not liking baby dolls any more than he understood her liking airplanes. He would never understand anything.

"Don't worry, darling," her mother said, but Pip was not reassured.

She went upstairs to her room and sat down at her desk. A picture of Al Wilson riding the lower wing of a speeding biplane lay on it. More forcefully than before the glossy photograph appeared to her for what it was, a flat piece of paper printed with a picture of motion which did not move. It was not real. She sat back in her chair and stared at it. Stills, Mr. Zick called the photographs sometimes, and that's what they were. They were not the same as the movie, and now the movie faded before what she imagined a real air circus to be. She saw herself standing at the edge of an open stubble field, her arm raised to shade her eyes as she watched a little plane flown by a real aviatrix in the blue sky above her. That would be real, and she would be there. Radyar knew; he understood, and he had promised to take her. Nothing, no one, not even her father, could stop Radyar from taking her. He couldn't, he couldn't, she told herself, feeling more and more that possibly he could.

A day later she found her mother seated at the writing desk in the living room and asked if she had written to her father.

"I am writing now, Pip," she said. "Don't worry. I am explaining about Radyar. Your father doesn't know anyone like him. Once he understands, everything will be all right. Don't worry." And she smiled and stretched out a curl on Pip's head. "Oh, your hair, darling."

At her first opportunity Pip walked to the Steadman drugstore after school with Marjorie. Barian rode his bike alongside in the street and called them names until Pip ran at him with her head down, but he pumped out of range. Instead of going into the drugstore she walked the five blocks to the Livingstones' and went around in back. Before she reached Radyar's open door, his voice called out, "Is that Pip approaching?" He was sitting at his drawing board and turned, smiling, toward the door.

"Hello, Radyar," she said. "How did you know it was me?"

"I heard small feet falling close together sounding very determined," and he laughed.

She stood beside the tilted drawing board and looked at the compass and drawing pencils and instruments and at the lines and circles on the paper. Now that Radyar didn't stick his hair down, it was dark brown, not black, and a little curly. She liked it better.

"Are you making a horoscope chart?"

"Yes," he said, dipping a pen in red ink and quickly

drawing a little monoplane in one corner. "It is the one I told you about, for the aviatrix in the air circus."

For a few minutes Pip didn't speak, watching him make quick little drawings in the corners of the paper. "Radyar, are we going to the air circus?"

"Of course." He finished sketching. "Why do you ask me that?" He looked at her steadily and then laughed. "You want to go. I want to go." He pulled the morning newspaper from the wastebasket. "Listen to this," and he read,

> "Four hundred planes to parade over San Diego. Two hundred more will be on exhibition. Squadron of army and navy ships joins in great air spectacle.

"This will be the greatest air show ever held anywhere." He dropped the paper into the basket again. "And I have business there, too," he said. "This horoscope." Suddenly he smiled directly at her. "Trust me, Pip."

A long sigh escaped her lips. She knew then that she would go to the air circus. Radyar was stronger and closer than her father. She could put her anxiety aside. After looking at him a moment, she held out her hand and they shook. "Good-bye, Radyar."

"Good-bye, Pip."

Rounding the corner of the Lower School the next day she saw the whole class clustered at the chicken coop. No one spoke or looked her way. She pressed closer to the wire. Mr. Romero stood inside the chicken yard, and in his brown palm he held an egg.

"Watch this," he said.

Resting on his palm the egg began to teeter. Then the shell cracked, the cracks widened, and the tip of a beak appeared in the exact center of the cracks.

"I see it!" Marjorie Steadman squealed. The other voices rose like Saturday afternoon at the movies. More and more of the beak appeared. The shell suddenly cracked in half, and a raw wet baby chick stood in Mr. Romero's palm.

"Oh, my goodness," said Miss Sixe, "isn't this exciting?"

Pip pressed up to the wire and watched Mr. Romero set the baby chick on its uncertain feet on the ground. In a moment the chick shook out its yellow fluff to dry and began to search through the dust for grain. How did it know, Pip wondered, when it had so recently been an egg? Before long there were half a dozen baby chicks cheeping and pecking over the dusty yard. Watching them, Pip thought, they know they are chickens right away. They were dumb and they were machines for laying eggs, and they couldn't fly but there was more to being a chicken than that.

"They don't look any different," Barian said. "They look just like the ones we bought."

"We'll have to wait and see when they get their first feathers," Miss Sixe said. "We will tell then, if the chicks will look like the rooster or like the hens or like a mixture of the two."

"There is more good news today," Miss Sixe said. "The doctors decided not to remove the muscles in Harold's thigh. He does have a brace on that leg, and he walks with crutches, but his mother says that he may be able to walk alone again."

"I knew he'd be all right," Pip said.

Everybody laughed at her, and Barian jeered, "You did not."

Pip felt her anger rise, and she thought of giving him a good butt in the stomach, but she had known since the day of the fire. She had known so clearly that she didn't bother to say, "I did too," out loud.

All day she thought of how she would teach Harold to walk again. She had seen Rin Tin Tin's master teach the great dog to use his leg again after it had been paralyzed in a brave rescue, and she saw herself doing the same, although she knew Rinty had been acting his part in the movie. Still she saw herself so clearly trying and trying until Harold dropped his crutches and stumbled toward her that she did not notice for a moment that she had entered her own house again and that her mother had turned a frightened face toward her. A second yellow telegram was in her hand. Pip stopped as if a wall of air held her back. Then she cried out, "Mother! can I go with Radyar?"

Her mother lifted the yellow paper and read:

I REPEAT I FORBID YOU TO ALLOW PIP TO ACCOM-
PANY THE MAN RADYAR STOP DETECTIVE INVESTI-
GATING HIS PAST NOW STOP I ARRIVE MAY 30 TO
TAKE PIP AND PARKMAN TO KANSAS CITY STOP
PLEASE HAVE THEM READY.

"No!" Pip screamed. "No."

Her mother came toward her, holding out her arms, but Pip dashed behind the sofa and stood alone.

"Oh, darling, I am sure it will be all right."

"NO! NO!" Pip's chest heaved and her throat was too tight to allow any sound but a scream. "Radyar's taking me to the air circus. He is! He is!"

"Oh, darling," her mother cried. "I tried to persuade him, to tell him, but — but — Pip, we don't know. We may be wrong about Radyar. Perhaps he has done something in the past, something quite harmful. We don't know."

"No!" Pip screamed. "It's not true. I know it isn't. I won't go back to Kansas City. I won't! I won't!"

"Oh, Pip, I am afraid you must."

"I won't! He can't make me!"

"But he can."

"Mother, you won't let him!"

"Oh, Pip, Pip."

"But you won't! You won't!"

"He can get lawyers, and he can take you away from me forever."

Pip clutched the back of the sofa and held on as the room rocked violently. Her breath would not come, and she could not speak.

"Pip," her mother whispered, "don't look at me like that."

# 🖣 21 🖢

## The Time Comes

HER HEAD was empty. It felt like a balloon filled with no thought, nothing but air. She sat at her desk for a long time without knowing how long. The first thing she noticed was the garage roof. She did not know how long she had looked at it through her window before she saw that it was empty. The basin of water had dried up, and the turtle was gone. She wondered how long it had been gone and if Parkman knew. She must tell him since it was his turtle. When she found Parkman and told him, he already knew. The turtle had been gone for two weeks, he said, and Pip was suddenly bewildered.

"You could have told me," she said.

"You could have looked out your window," Parkman said, which was true. She couldn't understand how she had missed it.

"I'll get your pictures for you," she said.

"I don't want any more," Parkman said.

"Aren't you going to make a collection anymore?"

"Maybe I am and maybe I'm not."

Pip went to the garage and got out her wagon. Standing in the drive, she realized that she didn't need the wagon if

[194]

she didn't bring back Parkman's collection. She looked at the helmet and goggles lying in the wagon bed, and after a minute she parked the wagon under the oak and walked down the drive.

The glass windows under the marquee of the Valley Paramount stood open, and Mr. Zick removed the thumbtacks with his pocket knife and set the old pictures aside and shined the new photographs on his sleeve before he tacked them up. Pip stood in silence beside him while he worked. When Mr. Zick looked around, he said, "All by yourself today? The airplane need to be refueled?"

"Parkman doesn't want any more pictures," she said.

Mr. Zick put four tacks into a coming attraction. "So that is Parkman's business. How's about the young lady?"

Pip didn't answer because she was not sure. The pictures were only pictures. They were not the real thing.

"Are you feeling better?"

Mr. Zick thumped his chest and wheezed once. "Not too bad for springtime. It could be worse. Come in my office and take the Al Wilson pix, before Mrs. Huckaby gives the place a spring cleaning." He laughed until he wheezed a little. "It could use it."

Pip knelt beside the piles of old pictures stacked against the office wall. She found four stunt pictures, one of a barrel roll, one a loop-the-loop, one a nose dive in flames and the fourth with Al Wilson riding the lower wing of a biplane. When she had found the four, she had enough.

"I am going to Kansas City as soon as school is out. My father is coming for me and Parkman."

"So soon? And I haven't one airplane picture coming up," said Mr. Zick. "That picture *Wings* I told you about. I am still trying to get it. Maybe I can book it for September when you come back."

Pip nodded. "Thank you, Mr. Zick." She held out her hand. "I guess I won't see you before I go."

"Good-bye, little Pip. This valley will not be the same without you." They shook hands, and Pip picked up her handful of photographs and left Mr. Zick's office.

At the post office corner she hesitated. The bell struck eleven o'clock, sounding so close that it might have been in her head. Afterward, she turned toward home. She would not go to see Radyar. Thinking of what her father might do, she was angry but she was also afraid. Then a picture of Harold gathered in her head. Instead of going home, she turned the opposite direction.

Harold's house was beyond the park where Yamaji had spoken in the amphitheater. It was a small white stucco house with a red tile roof and a small arched front doorway. Pip wondered if the door itself was arched on top, but when it opened, she saw that it wasn't.

"Why, hello, Ann Margaret." Harold's mother stood in the doorway. She had gray hair and she was old and she looked terribly tired. It surprised Pip that anyone had an old mother, and she thought no wonder Harold looked sad all the time.

"Is Harold coming home soon?" she asked.

"It will be next month." His mother's face brightened a little. "The middle of June, we hope."

Pip said nothing for a minute. "I am going to Kansas City May thirtieth. I'll be gone all summer."

"I'll tell Harold you were here. He will be so glad. I hope you will write to him. Your letters have made him so happy all these months."

Pip nodded. "I'll write him lots of times. Every time I think of it." She was certain it would be often.

Walking home she felt very tired and the pictures weighed heavily on her arm. When the little red roadster pulled up beside her and her mother smiled from behind the wheel, "May I give you a lift?" as if she were a stranger, she climbed in beside her without a word.

"I saw Radyar at the Livingstones' this morning."

Pip stared straight ahead.

"I explained the situation to him, and he understands and sends you his love."

There was a silence which Pip did not break.

"He has finished the aviatrix's horoscope now, and he will take it to her in San Diego. He promised to give me a complete description of the air circus so that you will feel as if you had been there."

Only being there would be like being there. She stared straight ahead.

"Pip, try to understand, darling. It is the best we can do."

She didn't reply to this and remained silent until her mother turned the car into the drive. Then she said, "Did you ask him if he did something bad?"

"No, no, I didn't. I couldn't. Oh, Pip, it seems so unlikely."

Getting out of the roadster, Pip said nothing. Everything, she felt, was coming to an end. She knew it in her heart. Everything around her carried the sense of ending. It did not surprise her at all that Miss Sixe addressed the semicircle of her pupils, saying, "Now that school is about to close, we will have to think of something to do with the chickens."

"Fry them!" Marjorie cried, and everyone shrieked with laughter, squealing, "I want a drumstick!"

Pip felt a shock. Those dumb, dirty chickens, still they didn't deserve to be killed. Suddenly she heard herself screaming, "No! No!" She jumped up, and she would have hit anyone near her to get their attention, but her blazing face commanded them. Barian caught himself between a laugh and a start. The others stared at her, their mouths open.

"Barian can take them home," she cried. "He lives on a ranch, and he already has a goat."

Barian's face lit up. "I can take them home. I'll build a house for them."

"They don't absolutely have to have a coop," said Miss Sixe. "But, Barian, I think you must talk it over with your parents."

Barian slumped a little as he said uncertainly, "They won't care."

"Well, they may, Barian. Chickens are a bit dirty. We know that."

Barian's parents did not mind at all. What were a few chickens added to the cattle and horses and dogs they already had, not to mention the angora goat?

A few days later Barian's father drove him to school in his pickup truck. It had chicken crates in the back. One by one the class went into the chicken coop and chased the hens until they caught them and stuffed them into the crates. Afterwards Mr. Romero secured the lids, and Mr. Nicholson pushed the crates back into the truck. Pip caught the rooster and felt a little sorry to see him go. Barian pursued the last two chicks, and he looked comical darting around the hen yard with his arms stretched out. When he finally got his hands on them, he bore them triumphantly to the truck. While his father packed them in the last crate and the class pressed around watching, Barian suddenly threw his arms around Pip and kissed her halfway on the mouth. The class shrieked with laughter and began to jeer. Miss Sixe and Mr. Romero and Mr. Nicholson smiled. Pip was too shocked to give Barian a shove. When he let her go and she stepped back in surprise, she saw Marjorie staring at her over Barian's shoulder. Barian grinned a little, wiping his mouth on the back of his hand.

After they had cleaned the coop for the last time, they prepared their reports on the chicken project which they were to read in front of the whole school on Parents' Day. Because she was the chairman of the chicken committee, Pip was to introduce each reader. Barian would read a report on building the coop. Marjorie prepared the financial statement, how much they had spent and how much they had earned from the eggs. It came out almost even.

Everyone in the school took part on the last day. Parkman memorized a poem, "The Ballad of John Silver." He learned it by heart standing in the doorway of his room and intoning the lines in a singsong voice:

*We were schooner-rigged and rakish,*
*with a long and lissome hull,*
*And we flew the pretty colors*
*of the cross-bones and the skull . . .*

After he stuck his tongue out of the corner of his mouth and thought very hard, the next line would come to him. Then he had to start all over to get the rhythm again.

Pip let him borrow her skull and rib bones for the recitation. They folded black cretonne around an orange crate and stuffed red tissue paper into the eye sockets of the skull. With a flashlight stuck behind it and turned on, it was the sensation of the final assembly. Everyone oohed and clapped before Parkman began, and he recited the poem all the way through, only stopping to think hard once.

Pip wore her blue dress with the embroidery and the silver buttons and the long sleeves and belt. Standing in front of the whole school made her heart race and the sweat sprang up in her hair, but she held her notebook open in front of her and it didn't shake much. She told the audience about the chickens, and she introduced each report. When she thought she was finished, she had forgotten Marjorie and Miss Sixe had to remind her. It made her mad at herself and Marjorie accused her later of doing it on purpose, but it was the only mistake she made. Her mother said she was sure no one ever noticed, and Aunt Andrea said she certainly hadn't, but Pip did not like making a mistake, not even an unnoticed one.

After the assembly there was a great picnic under the shade trees outside the main building. The parents found the hard-boiled eggs exceptionally good and mentioned them to the members of the chicken committee. Pip was happy.

When their telephone rang just before dinner that night, she heard it with a sudden shock. She stood very still and listened, and she heard her mother say, "Oh, hello, Edward." And after a silence, "Yes, they are ready." Another pause. "Tomorrow morning at nine o'clock? All right. We will expect you." Her mother hung the black receiver on the pronged lever which clicked as it went down. She set the upright black phone back on the black desk and turned to meet Pip's gaze.

For a long moment they looked into each other's eyes. Then her mother said, "Your father has arrived in the valley."

Pip knew that the time had come.

# ⧘ 22 ⧘

## Leaving the Valley

Pip lay in the iron bed on the sleeping porch, and her mother sat for a moment on the blue bedspread, her hand resting on the covers over Pip's folded hands.

"There is always something we can't do anything about, darling," she began and then fell silent. "It's like the woodpecker." Watching her, Pip said nothing.

For a long time after her mother had gone, Pip's eyes stayed open and sleepless. One solitary star hung in the gray gap among the sycamore leaves. She wasn't certain that she fell asleep the long night through, but once she found herself looking through the hole to the sky, three very small faraway stars were there and then it became not a hole but a scrap of transparent pale gray. She heard the woodpecker begin to drum on the tile roof over their heads and Parkman's bedsprings squeak as he turned over. Then she got up and padded into her room.

Her little straw suitcase had stayed on the floor of her wardrobe since she had returned to the house last September. Now she pulled it out and opened it. For a few moments she considered what she wanted to put in it. The skull and bones were too big. They were out of the question. She took down one Al Wilson picture and placed it on the bottom. She wondered if she should take her horoscope. If she did, she would have to fold it and then it would have creases across it forever afterwards to spoil the little drawings of crabs and scorpions and lions. She liked the great circle and the slices of pie cut in it for each animal like a strange little zoo and the pencil lines and thick black India ink drawings and Radyar's circular handwriting. She wished now that she hadn't put thumbtacks in the corners. It should be framed like a picture. Then she knew for certain that she did not want to crease it.

From her desk she took the last four pictures Mr. Zick had given her and laid them in the suitcase. On top of them she put a tablet and a box of crayons and two thick brown wood pencils and her book, *Boy's Story of Lindbergh*, which she had read three times since Parkman gave it to her for Christmas. She couldn't think of anything else. She closed the case and fastened it with the wooden pegs which dangled on strings from each closure, dressed in her blue embroidered dress and went downstairs to breakfast. Beside her place on the porch table Mrs. Hernandez had laid her helmet and goggles. Her mother's place, she noticed, had already been used. After a few minutes Parkman came out and sat down.

"I will miss you both," said Mrs. Hernandez, putting their glasses of orange juice before them. "The summers are lonesome without you."

Pip could not reply, staring in front of her. After a while she asked, "Parkman, are you all ready?"

"I guess so," Parkman said. "You can have my bacon." And Pip took one strip because he offered it, even though she did not feel like eating.

The big square-cornered leather suitcases stood ready by the front door. Leather straps were buckled around them. In the living room her mother walked from one long window to the other past the black writing desk. She glanced through each window to the drive before she turned to press her fingertips against her temples.

"Do you have a headache?"

Her mother smiled quickly. "Not very bad. He will be here any moment. Are you all ready?"

Pip nodded. "I packed my straw suitcase."

"I hope you put in enough things to play with on the trip. It will take three or four days to drive all the way to Kansas City. It's longer than by train."

"I can make up things," Pip said, and her mother stopped her pacing and smiled at her. "I know you can, darling, I know you can." Then she pressed her fingers to her temples and breathed deeply. At the same moment they heard heavy wheels turning on the drive, a motor throbbing and coming to a stop. A door creaked, then slammed. Her mother went to the door and placed her hand on the knob. Behind her Pip darted into the little bathroom under the stairs and held herself very still in the dark. The blood thumped against her ears. She wondered where the cockroach was, but she didn't dare turn on the light.

In a moment the front door opened, and the silence in the house changed to the silence between two people.

"Hello, Edward," she heard her mother say. And in reply she heard her father's voice say, "Hello, Dorrit," and she felt a thrill of recognition and fear.

"I hope they are ready. I want to get started. I am going to take them to Yosemite on the way back."

"How nice. They have never been there. Parkman particularly will like that."

"I know that," her father said. "Where are they?"

"Parkman went upstairs to finish his packing, and Pip was here a moment ago. I didn't see where she went."

"I hope she doesn't think she can hold us up."

"I am sure she doesn't, Edward. You know better than that."

"I wouldn't know what she has learned this winter."

Pip heard the wicker sofa creak as her father sat down in it in the thickening silence.

"Just what do you mean by that?" asked her mother.

"You know what I mean, Dorrit."

"No, Edward, I do not."

During the long silence Pip pressed her hands against her head to keep it from blowing apart.

"I mean the associations you permit your own young, impressionable daughter to have. It makes me wonder about your judgment as her mother."

Her mother's voice rose. "My judgment as her mother is perfectly good. Just what associations do you mean, anyway?"

"I mean your allowing this fake astrologer to play around with a little girl."

"Radyar is not a fake astrologer," cried her mother.

"There isn't any other kind!" her father shouted. "So he has you deceived, too. What is he, your boyfriend?"

"He is a very dear friend, but he is not what you think. He is not my boyfriend."

Her father snorted. "Well, I shall soon know all there is to know about him. My private detective has already discovered that five years ago he had to change his name."

With that Pip opened the bathroom door and stepped out. Her mother and her father stared at her in surprise, and her mother drew in her breath.

"Radyar's name was Hiram Joseph Smith, and he changed it because he didn't like it," Pip said. "I knew that all the time." Grasping the newel post she wheeled around it and fled up the stairs.

The silence behind her was so profound that she stopped before she slammed the door of her room.

"Edward," she heard her mother say, "if you wish to hurt me, then hurt me. Don't hurt her."

The stillness so thickened in the house that Pip shut her door without a sound. She leaned against it with her heart banging so painfully that the blood hurt in her ears. She surged with hatred for her father. How could she go downstairs and leave the house and get into the big touring car and drive away with him? How could she leave her mother behind? All of these things she must do and do in the next few minutes for fear that she might be separated from her mother and Radyar and the whole valley forever. "Fear crushes life," Radyar told her, and she knew it was true. Her fright made breathing difficult.

After a while she heard Parkman open his door and go downstairs. When she heard the front door open and close, she took her straw suitcase and went down the stairs. From behind the front door jamb she peeked out.

Her father and Parkman bent over the lefthand running board. The luggage rack stretched out like a string of x's from fender to fender. Her father clamped it to the running board while Parkman turned the screws which secured it to the fenders. Her father shook it to test its strength and gave added turns to Parkman's work. Then he lifted the huge square-cornered leather suitcase and set it upright behind the rack against the car door. Behind it so that it blocked the rear door he heaved the matching case, its dark leather scraped raw and yellow by the metal. Once the luggage was on, no one could get in the lefthand doors.

Parkman and their father circled the front end of the huge car. Her father glanced at the round glass thermometer on the radiator as he passed. "It's getting hot here in the sun. Where is she? Will you please tell her to hurry up?"

Her mother stood beside the drive. "She will come as soon as she's ready."

"And when will that be?"

"I'm sure she's coming, Edward."

Her mother put her arms around Parkman and hugged him and rested her cheek on the top of his head. "Have a good summer, darling. Take care of Pip for me. I'll be waiting for you here in September."

Her father pressed the horn in the center of the steering wheel several times. It made a hoarse ooo-ga ooo-ga.

Watching through the screen, Pip knew that she must go out. She gripped the straw suitcase and took a deep breath. At that moment Mrs. Hernandez came up beside her, and in her hand she held Pip's helmet and goggles.

"You left them on the table," she whispered. She bent to straighten the bow tie on Pip's belt as the telephone started ringing. Mrs. Hernandez picked up the black phone and spoke. "Yes . . . yes . . . I'll tell her . . . thank you." She came back to Pip by the door.

"That was Mr. Zick," she said. "He asked me to tell you he has booked *Wings* for the middle of September."

"Oh, Mrs. Hernandez!"

"Now you go." She gave Pip a little push through the door, and Pip emerged into the sunlight, her straw suitcase in one hand and her helmet and goggles in the other. The ooo-ga honking stopped.

"Good-bye, Mother," she said, lifting her face.

"Oh, Pip! Pip!"

"Don't worry. I'll be back in September."

Pip opened the door to the backseat, set her straw suitcase on the floor, and sat down on the edge of the hot leather cushion. Her mother covered her cheeks with kisses.

"Don't worry, Mother," she said.

"Oh, Pip, darling." She closed the door and stepped back. Pip pulled her helmet over her curly head. When she had it fastened under her chin, she stuffed the lingering wisps up under the edges and hooked the elastic around the back of her head and settled the little round goggles over her eyes.

"Oh, Pip!" Her mother pressed the back of her hand to her lips.

"Contact, let 'er go," Pip said. Her mother made a gesture of pulling the blocks away and stepped back. As the great touring car rolled down the driveway, Pip raised her arm in salute and her mother returned it.